I0831631

SENSE AND SENSIBILITY

VOLUME ONE OF TWO

Sense and Sensibility

Austen, Jane 1775 – 1817

First Published by Thomas Egerton in 1811

Text set in 18 point Helvetica.
Chapter headings set in Helvetica Neue.

ISBN: 978-1-83412-378-3 Volume One
ISBN: 978-1-83412-379-0 Volume Two

SENSE AND SENSIBILITY

VOLUME ONE OF TWO

GRAND TYPE CLASSICS

Jane Austen

CONTENTS

Sense and Sensibility

VOLUME ONE

Chapter One **9**
Chapter Two **19**
Chapter Three **31**
Chapter Four **41**
Chapter Five **54**
Chapter Six **61**
Chapter Seven **70**
Chapter Eight **79**
Chapter Nine **87**
Chapter Ten **99**
Chapter Eleven **113**
Chapter Twelve **123**
Chapter Thirteen **134**
Chapter Fourteen **148**
Chapter Fifteen **158**
Chapter Sixteen **175**

Chapter Seventeen **189**
Chapter Eighteen **200**
Chapter Nineteen **210**
Chapter Twenty **228**
Chapter Twenty One **243**
Chapter Twenty Two **262**
Chapter Twenty Three **280**
Chapter Twenty Four **295**
Chapter Twenty Five **309**
Chapter Twenty Six **321**
Chapter Twenty Seven **337**
Chapter Twenty Eight **353**
Chapter Twenty Nine **363**
Chapter Thirty **387**

VOLUME TWO

Chapter Thirty One **405**
Chapter Thirty Two **428**
Chapter Thirty Three **445**
Chapter Thirty Four **464**
Chapter Thirty Five **481**
Chapter Thirty Six **496**

Chapter Thirty Seven **515**
Chapter Thirty Eight **542**
Chapter Thirty Nine **560**
Chapter Fourty **573**
Chapter Fourty One **589**
Chapter Fourty Two **606**
Chapter Fourty Three **618**
Chapter Fourty Four **640**
Chapter Fourty Five **673**
Chapter Fourty Six **687**
Chapter Fourty Seven **705**
Chapter Fourty Eight **721**
Chapter Fourty Nine **730**
Chapter Fifty **756**

CHAPTER ONE

THE FAMILY OF DASHWOOD had long been settled in Sussex. Their estate was large, and their residence was at Norland Park, in the centre of their property, where, for many generations, they had lived in so respectable a manner as to engage the general good opinion of their surrounding acquaintance. The late owner of this estate was a single man, who lived to a very advanced age, and who for many years of his life, had a constant companion and housekeeper in his sister. But her death, which happened ten years before his own, produced a great alteration in his home; for to supply her loss, he invited and received into his house the family of his nephew Mr. Henry Dashwood, the legal inheritor of the Norland estate, and the person to whom he intended to bequeath it. In the society of his nephew and niece, and their children, the old Gentleman's days were comfortably spent. His attachment to them all increased. The constant attention of Mr. and Mrs. Henry Dashwood to his wishes, which proceeded not merely from interest, but from goodness of heart, gave him every degree of solid comfort which his age could receive; and the cheerfulness of the children added a relish to his existence.

By a former marriage, Mr. Henry Dashwood had one son: by his present lady, three daughters. The son, a steady respectable young man, was amply provided for by the fortune of his mother, which had been large, and half of which devolved on him on his coming of age. By his own marriage, likewise, which happened soon afterwards, he added to his wealth. To him therefore the succession to the Norland estate was not so really important as to his sisters; for their fortune, independent of what might arise to them from their father's inheriting that property, could be but small. Their mother had nothing, and their father only seven thousand pounds in his own disposal; for the remaining moiety of his first wife's fortune was also secured to her child, and he had only a life-interest in it.

The old gentleman died: his will was read, and like almost every other will, gave as much disappointment as pleasure. He was neither so unjust, nor so ungrateful, as to leave his estate from his nephew; – but he left it to him on such terms as destroyed half the value of the bequest. Mr. Dashwood had wished for it more for the sake of his wife and daughters than for himself or his son; –

but to his son, and his son's son, a child of four years old, it was secured, in such a way, as to leave to himself no power of providing for those who were most dear to him, and who most needed a provision by any charge on the estate, or by any sale of its valuable woods. The whole was tied up for the benefit of this child, who, in occasional visits with his father and mother at Norland, had so far gained on the affections of his uncle, by such attractions as are by no means unusual in children of two or three years old; an imperfect articulation, an earnest desire of having his own way, many cunning tricks, and a great deal of noise, as to outweigh all the value of all the attention which, for years, he had received from his niece and her daughters. He meant not to be unkind, however, and, as a mark of his affection for the three girls, he left them a thousand pounds a-piece.

Mr. Dashwood's disappointment was, at first, severe; but his temper was cheerful and sanguine; and he might reasonably hope to live many years, and by living economically, lay by a considerable sum from the produce of an estate already large, and capable of almost immediate improvement. But the fortune, which had been so tardy in coming, was his only one twelvemonth. He survived his uncle no longer; and ten thousand pounds, including the late legacies, was all that remained for his widow and daughters.

His son was sent for as soon as his danger was known, and to him Mr. Dashwood recommended, with all the strength and urgency which illness could command, the interest of his mother-in-law and sisters.

Mr. John Dashwood had not the strong feelings of the rest of the family; but he was affected by a recommendation of such a nature at such a time, and he promised to do every thing in his power to make them comfortable. His father was rendered easy by such an assurance, and Mr. John Dashwood had then leisure to consider how much there might prudently be in his power to do for them.

He was not an ill-disposed young man, unless to be rather cold hearted and rather selfish is to be ill-disposed: but he was, in general, well respected; for he conducted himself with propriety in the discharge of his ordinary duties. Had he married a more amiable woman, he might have been made still more respectable than he was: – he might even have been made amiable himself; for he was very young when he married, and very fond of his wife. But Mrs. John Dashwood was a strong caricature of himself; – more narrow-minded and selfish.

When he gave his promise to his father, he meditated within himself to increase the fortunes of his sisters by the present of a thousand pounds a-piece. He then really thought himself equal to it. The prospect of four thousand a-year, in addition to his present income, besides the remaining half of his own mother's fortune, warmed his heart, and made him feel capable of generosity. – "Yes, he would give them three thousand pounds: it would be liberal and handsome! It would be enough to make them completely easy. Three thousand pounds! he could spare so considerable a sum with little inconvenience." – He thought of it all day long, and for many days successively, and he did not repent.

No sooner was his father's funeral over, than Mrs. John Dashwood, without sending any notice of her intention to her mother-in-law, arrived with her child and their attendants. No one could dispute her right to come; the house was her husband's from the moment of his father's decease; but the indelicacy of her conduct was so much the greater, and to a woman in Mrs. Dashwood's situation, with only common feelings, must have been highly unpleasing; – but in **her** mind there was a sense of honor so keen, a generosity so romantic, that any offence of the kind, by whomsoever given or received, was to her a source of immovable disgust.

Mrs. John Dashwood had never been a favourite with any of her husband's family; but she had had no opportunity, till the present, of shewing them with how little attention to the comfort of other people she could act when occasion required it.

So acutely did Mrs. Dashwood feel this ungracious behaviour, and so earnestly did she despise her daughter-in-law for it, that, on the arrival of the latter, she would have quitted the house for ever, had not the entreaty of her eldest girl induced her first to reflect on the propriety of going, and her own tender love for all her three children determined her afterwards to stay, and for their sakes avoid a breach with their brother.

Elinor, this eldest daughter, whose advice was so effectual, possessed a strength of understanding, and coolness of judgment, which qualified her, though only nineteen, to be the counsellor of her mother, and enabled her frequently to counteract, to the advantage of them all, that eagerness of mind in Mrs. Dashwood which must generally have led to imprudence. She had an excellent heart; – her disposition was affectionate, and her feelings were strong; but she knew how to govern them: it was a knowledge which her mother had yet to learn; and which one of her sisters had resolved never to be taught.

Marianne's abilities were, in many respects, quite equal to Elinor's. She was sensible and clever; but eager in everything: her sorrows, her joys, could have no moderation. She was generous, amiable, interesting: she was everything but prudent. The resemblance between her and her mother was strikingly great.

Elinor saw, with concern, the excess of her sister's sensibility; but by Mrs. Dashwood it was valued and cherished. They encouraged each other now in the violence of their affliction. The agony of grief which overpowered them at first, was voluntarily renewed, was sought for, was created again and again. They gave themselves up wholly to their sorrow, seeking increase of wretchedness in every reflection that could afford it, and resolved against ever admitting consolation in future. Elinor, too, was deeply afflicted; but still she could struggle, she could exert herself. She could consult with her brother, could receive her sister-in-law on her arrival, and treat her with proper attention; and could strive to rouse her mother to similar exertion, and encourage her to similar forbearance.

Margaret, the other sister, was a good-humored, well-disposed girl; but as she had already imbibed a good deal of Marianne's romance, without having much of her sense, she did not, at thirteen, bid fair to equal her sisters at a more advanced period of life.

CHAPTER TWO

MRS. JOHN DASHWOOD now installed herself mistress of Norland; and her mother and sisters-in-law were degraded to the condition of visitors. As such, however, they were treated by her with quiet civility; and by her husband with as much kindness as he could feel towards anybody beyond himself, his wife, and their child. He really pressed them, with some earnestness, to consider Norland as their home; and, as no plan appeared so eligible to Mrs. Dashwood as remaining there till she could accommodate herself with a house in the neighbourhood, his invitation was accepted.

A continuance in a place where everything reminded her of former delight, was exactly what suited her mind. In seasons of cheerfulness, no temper could be more cheerful than hers, or possess, in a greater degree, that sanguine expectation of happiness which is happiness itself. But in sorrow she must be equally carried away by her fancy, and as far beyond consolation as in pleasure she was beyond alloy.

Mrs. John Dashwood did not at all approve of what her husband intended to do for his sisters. To take three thousand pounds from the fortune of their dear little boy would be impoverishing him to the most dreadful degree. She begged him to think again on the subject. How could he answer it to himself to rob his child, and his only child too, of so large a sum? And what possible claim could the Miss Dashwoods, who were related to him only by half blood, which she considered as no relationship at all, have on his generosity to so large an amount. It was very well known that no affection was ever supposed to exist between the children of any man by different marriages; and why was he to ruin himself, and their poor little Harry, by giving away all his money to his half sisters?

"It was my father's last request to me," replied her husband, "that I should assist his widow and daughters."

"He did not know what he was talking of, I dare say; ten to one but he was light-headed at the time. Had he been in his right senses, he could not have thought of such a thing as begging you to give away half your fortune from your own child."

"He did not stipulate for any particular sum, my dear Fanny; he only requested me, in general terms, to assist them, and make their situation more comfortable than it was in his power to do. Perhaps it would have been as well if he had left it wholly to myself. He could hardly suppose I should neglect them. But as he required the promise, I could not do less than give it; at least I thought so at the time. The promise, therefore, was given, and must be performed. Something must be done for them whenever they leave Norland and settle in a new home."

"Well, then, **let** something be done for them; but **that** something need not be three thousand pounds. Consider," she added, "that when the money is once parted with, it never can return. Your sisters will marry, and it will be gone for ever. If, indeed, it could be restored to our poor little boy – "

"Why, to be sure," said her husband, very gravely, "that would make great difference. The time may come when Harry will regret that so large a sum was parted with. If he should have a numerous family, for instance, it would be a very convenient addition."

"To be sure it would."

"Perhaps, then, it would be better for all

parties, if the sum were diminished one half. – Five hundred pounds would be a prodigious increase to their fortunes!"

"Oh! beyond anything great! What brother on earth would do half so much for his sisters, even if **really** his sisters! And as it is – only half blood! – But you have such a generous spirit!"

"I would not wish to do any thing mean," he replied. "One had rather, on such occasions, do too much than too little. No one, at least, can think I have not done enough for them: even themselves, they can hardly expect more."

"There is no knowing what **they** may expect," said the lady, "but we are not to think of their expectations: the question is, what you can afford to do."

"Certainly – and I think I may afford to give them five hundred pounds a-piece. As it is, without any addition of mine, they will each have about three thousand pounds on their mother's death – a very comfortable fortune for any young woman."

"To be sure it is; and, indeed, it strikes me that they can want no addition at all. They will have ten thousand pounds divided amongst them. If they marry, they will be sure of doing well, and if they do not, they may all live very comfortably together on the interest of ten thousand pounds."

"That is very true, and, therefore, I do not know whether, upon the whole, it would not be more advisable to do something for their mother while she lives, rather than for them – something of the annuity kind I mean. – My sisters would feel the good effects of it as well as herself. A hundred a year would make them all perfectly comfortable."

His wife hesitated a little, however, in giving her consent to this plan.

"To be sure," said she, "it is better than parting with fifteen hundred pounds at once. But, then, if Mrs. Dashwood should live fifteen years we shall be completely taken in."

"Fifteen years! my dear Fanny; her life cannot be worth half that purchase."

"Certainly not; but if you observe, people always live for ever when there is an annuity to be paid them; and she is very stout and healthy, and hardly forty. An annuity is a very serious business; it comes over and over every year, and there is no getting rid of it. You are not aware of what you are doing. I have known a great deal of the trouble of annuities; for my mother was clogged with the payment of three to old superannuated servants by my father's will, and it is amazing how disagreeable she found it. Twice every year these annuities were to be paid; and then there was the trouble of getting it to them; and then one of them was said to have died, and afterwards it turned out to be no such thing. My mother was quite sick of it. Her income was not her own, she said, with such perpetual claims on it; and it was the more unkind in my father, because, otherwise, the money would have been entirely at my mother's disposal, without any restriction whatever. It has given me such an abhorrence of annuities, that I am sure I would not pin myself down to the payment of one for all the world."

"It is certainly an unpleasant thing," replied Mr. Dashwood, "to have those kind of yearly drains on one's income. One's fortune, as your mother justly says, is **not** one's own. To be tied down to the regular payment of such a sum, on every rent day, is by no means desirable: it takes away one's independence."

"Undoubtedly; and after all you have no thanks for it. They think themselves secure, you do no more than what is expected, and it raises no gratitude at all. If I were you, whatever I did should be done at my own discretion entirely. I would not bind myself to allow them any thing yearly. It may be very inconvenient some years to spare a hundred, or even fifty pounds from our own expenses."

"I believe you are right, my love; it will be better that there should be no annuity in the case; whatever I may give them occasionally will be of far greater assistance than a yearly allowance, because they would only enlarge their style of living if they felt sure of a larger income, and would not be sixpence the richer for it at the end of the year. It will certainly be much the best way. A present of fifty pounds, now and then, will prevent their ever being distressed for money, and will, I think, be amply discharging my promise to my father."

"To be sure it will. Indeed, to say the truth, I am convinced within myself that your father had no idea of your giving them any money at all. The assistance he thought of, I dare say, was only such as might be reasonably expected of you; for instance, such as looking out for a comfortable small house for them, helping them to move their things, and sending them presents of fish and game, and so forth, whenever they are in season. I'll lay my life that he meant nothing farther; indeed, it would be very strange and unreasonable if he did. Do but consider, my dear Mr. Dashwood, how excessively comfortable your mother-in-law and her daughters may live on the interest of seven thousand pounds, besides the thousand pounds belonging to each of the girls, which brings them in fifty pounds a year a-piece, and, of course, they will pay their mother for their board out of it. Altogether, they will have five hundred a-year amongst them, and what on earth can four women want for more than that? – They will live so cheap! Their housekeeping will be nothing at all. They will have no carriage, no horses, and hardly any servants; they will keep no company, and can have no expenses of any kind! Only conceive how comfortable they will be! Five hundred a year! I am sure I cannot imagine how they will spend half of it; and as to your giving them more, it is quite absurd to think of it. They will be much more able to give **you** something."

"Upon my word," said Mr. Dashwood, "I believe you are perfectly right. My father certainly could mean nothing more by his request to me than what you say. I clearly understand it now, and I will strictly fulfil my engagement by such acts of assistance and kindness to them as you have described. When my mother removes into another house my services shall be readily given to accommodate her as far as I can. Some little present of furniture too may be acceptable then."

"Certainly," returned Mrs. John Dashwood. "But, however, **one** thing must be considered. When your father and mother moved to Norland, though the furniture of Stanhill was sold, all the china, plate, and linen was saved, and is now left to your mother. Her house will therefore be almost completely fitted up as soon as she takes it."

"That is a material consideration undoubtedly. A valuable legacy indeed!

And yet some of the plate would have been a very pleasant addition to our own stock here."

"Yes; and the set of breakfast china is twice as handsome as what belongs to this house. A great deal too handsome, in my opinion, for any place **they** can ever afford to live in. But, however, so it is. Your father thought only of **them**. And I must say this: that you owe no particular gratitude to him, nor attention to his wishes; for we very well know that if he could, he would have left almost everything in the world to **them**."

This argument was irresistible. It gave to his intentions whatever of decision was wanting before; and he finally resolved, that it would be absolutely unnecessary, if not highly indecorous, to do more for the widow and children of his father, than such kind of neighbourly acts as his own wife pointed out.

CHAPTER THREE

MRS. DASHWOOD REMAINED at Norland several months; not from any disinclination to move when the sight of every well known spot ceased to raise the violent emotion which it produced for a while; for when her spirits began to revive, and her mind became capable of some other exertion than that of heightening its affliction by melancholy remembrances, she was impatient to be gone, and indefatigable in her inquiries for a suitable dwelling in the neighbourhood of

Norland; for to remove far from that beloved spot was impossible. But she could hear of no situation that at once answered her notions of comfort and ease, and suited the prudence of her eldest daughter, whose steadier judgment rejected several houses as too large for their income, which her mother would have approved.

Mrs. Dashwood had been informed by her husband of the solemn promise on the part of his son in their favour, which gave comfort to his last earthly reflections. She doubted the sincerity of this assurance no more than he had doubted it himself, and she thought of it for her daughters' sake with satisfaction, though as for herself she was persuaded that a much smaller provision than 7000L would support her in affluence. For their brother's sake, too, for the sake of his own heart, she rejoiced; and she reproached herself for being unjust to his merit before, in believing him incapable of generosity. His attentive behaviour to herself and his sisters convinced her that their welfare was dear to him, and, for a long time, she firmly relied on the liberality of his intentions.

The contempt which she had, very early in their acquaintance, felt for her daughter-in-law, was very much increased by the farther knowledge of her character, which half a year's residence in her family afforded; and perhaps in spite of every consideration of politeness or maternal affection on the side of the former, the two ladies might have found it impossible to have lived together so long, had not a particular circumstance occurred to give still greater eligibility, according to the opinions of Mrs. Dashwood, to her daughters' continuance at Norland.

This circumstance was a growing attachment between her eldest girl and the brother of Mrs. John Dashwood, a gentleman-like and pleasing young man, who was introduced to their acquaintance soon after his sister's establishment at

Norland, and who had since spent the greatest part of his time there.

Some mothers might have encouraged the intimacy from motives of interest, for Edward Ferrars was the eldest son of a man who had died very rich; and some might have repressed it from motives of prudence, for, except a trifling sum, the whole of his fortune depended on the will of his mother. But Mrs. Dashwood was alike uninfluenced by either consideration. It was enough for her that he appeared to be amiable, that he loved her daughter, and that Elinor returned the partiality. It was contrary to every doctrine of hers that difference of fortune should keep any couple asunder who were attracted by resemblance of disposition; and that Elinor's merit should not be acknowledged by every one who knew her, was to her comprehension impossible.

Edward Ferrars was not recommended to their good opinion by any peculiar graces of person or address. He was not handsome, and his manners required intimacy to make them pleasing. He was too diffident to do justice to himself; but when his natural shyness was overcome, his behaviour gave every indication of an open, affectionate heart. His understanding was good, and his education had given it solid improvement. But he was neither fitted by abilities nor disposition to answer the wishes of his mother and sister, who longed to see him distinguished – as – they hardly knew what. They wanted him to make a fine figure in the world in some manner or other. His mother wished to interest him in political concerns, to get him into parliament, or to see him connected with some of the great men of the day. Mrs. John Dashwood wished it likewise; but in the mean while, till one of these superior blessings could be attained, it would have quieted her ambition to see him driving a barouche. But Edward had no turn for great men or barouches. All his wishes centered in domestic comfort and the quiet of private life. Fortunately he had a younger brother who was more promising.

Edward had been staying several weeks in the house before he engaged much of Mrs. Dashwood's attention; for she was, at that time, in such affliction as rendered her careless of surrounding objects. She saw only that he was quiet and unobtrusive, and she liked him for it. He did not disturb the wretchedness of her mind by ill-timed conversation. She was first called to observe and approve him farther, by a reflection which Elinor chanced one day to make on the difference between him and his sister. It was a contrast which recommended him most forcibly to her mother.

"It is enough," said she; "to say that he is unlike Fanny is enough. It implies everything amiable. I love him already."

"I think you will like him," said Elinor, "when you know more of him."

"Like him!" replied her mother with a smile. "I feel no sentiment of approbation inferior to love."

"You may esteem him."

"I have never yet known what it was to separate esteem and love."

Mrs. Dashwood now took pains to get acquainted with him. Her manners were attaching, and soon banished his reserve. She speedily comprehended all his merits; the persuasion of his regard for Elinor perhaps assisted her penetration; but she really felt assured of his worth: and even that quietness of manner, which militated against all her established ideas of what a young man's address ought to be, was no longer uninteresting when she knew his heart to be warm and his temper affectionate.

No sooner did she perceive any symptom of love in his behaviour to Elinor, than she considered their serious attachment as certain, and looked forward to their marriage as rapidly approaching.

"In a few months, my dear Marianne." said she, "Elinor will, in all probability be settled for life. We shall miss her; but **she** will be happy."

"Oh! Mama, how shall we do without her?"

"My love, it will be scarcely a separation. We shall live within a few miles of each other, and shall meet every day of our lives. You will gain a brother, a real, affectionate brother. I have the highest opinion in the world of Edward's heart. But you look grave, Marianne; do you disapprove your sister's choice?"

"Perhaps," said Marianne, "I may consider it with some surprise. Edward is very amiable, and I love him tenderly. But yet – he is not the kind of young man – there is something wanting – his figure is not striking; it has none of that grace which I should expect in the man who could seriously attach my sister. His eyes want all that spirit, that fire, which at once announce virtue and intelligence. And besides all this, I am afraid, Mama, he has no real taste. Music seems scarcely to attract him, and though he admires Elinor's drawings very much, it is not the admiration of a person who can understand their worth. It is evident, in spite of his frequent attention to her while she draws, that in fact he knows nothing of the matter. He admires as a lover, not as a connoisseur. To satisfy me, those characters must be united. I could not be happy with a man whose taste did not in every point coincide with my own. He must enter into all my feelings; the same books, the same music must charm us both. Oh! mama, how spiritless, how tame was Edward's manner in reading to us last night! I felt for my sister most severely. Yet she bore it with so much composure, she seemed scarcely to notice it. I could hardly keep my seat. To hear those beautiful lines which have frequently almost driven me wild, pronounced with such impenetrable calmness, such dreadful indifference!"

"He would certainly have done more justice to simple and elegant prose. I thought so at the time; but you **would** give him Cowper."

"Nay, Mama, if he is not to be animated by Cowper! – but we must allow for difference of taste. Elinor has not my feelings, and therefore she may overlook it, and be happy with him. But it would have broke **my** heart, had I loved him, to hear him read with so little sensibility. Mama, the more I know of the world, the more am I convinced that I shall never see a man whom I can really love. I require so much! He must have all Edward's virtues, and his person and manners must ornament his goodness with every possible charm."

"Remember, my love, that you are not seventeen. It is yet too early in life to despair of such a happiness. Why should you be less fortunate than your mother? In one circumstance only, my Marianne, may your destiny be different from hers!"

CHAPTER FOUR

WHAT A PITY IT IS, Elinor," said Marianne, "that Edward should have no taste for drawing."

"No taste for drawing!" replied Elinor, "why should you think so? He does not draw himself, indeed, but he has great pleasure in seeing the performances of other people, and I assure you he is by no means deficient in natural taste, though he has not had opportunities of improving it. Had he ever been in the way of learning, I think he would have drawn very well. He distrusts his own judgment in such matters so much, that he is always unwilling to give his opinion on any picture; but he has an innate propriety and simplicity of taste, which in general direct him perfectly right."

Marianne was afraid of offending, and said no more on the subject; but the kind of approbation which Elinor described as excited in him by the drawings of other people, was very far from that rapturous delight, which, in her opinion, could alone be called taste. Yet, though smiling within herself at the mistake, she honoured her sister for that blind partiality to Edward which produced it.

"I hope, Marianne," continued Elinor, "you do not consider him as deficient in general taste. Indeed, I think I may say that you cannot, for your behaviour to him is perfectly cordial, and if **that** were your opinion, I am sure you could never be civil to him."

Marianne hardly knew what to say. She

would not wound the feelings of her sister on any account, and yet to say what she did not believe was impossible. At length she replied:

"Do not be offended, Elinor, if my praise of him is not in every thing equal to your sense of his merits. I have not had so many opportunities of estimating the minuter propensities of his mind, his inclinations and tastes, as you have; but I have the highest opinion in the world of his goodness and sense. I think him every thing that is worthy and amiable."

"I am sure," replied Elinor, with a smile, "that his dearest friends could not be dissatisfied with such commendation as that. I do not perceive how you could express yourself more warmly."

Marianne was rejoiced to find her sister so easily pleased.

"Of his sense and his goodness," continued Elinor, "no one can, I think, be in doubt, who has seen him often enough to engage him in unreserved conversation. The excellence of his understanding and his principles can be concealed only by that shyness which too often keeps him silent. You know enough of him to do justice to his solid worth. But of his minuter propensities, as you call them you have from peculiar circumstances been kept more ignorant than myself. He and I have been at times thrown a good deal together, while you have been wholly engrossed on the most affectionate principle by my mother. I have seen a great deal of him, have studied his sentiments and heard his opinion on subjects of literature and taste; and, upon the whole, I venture to pronounce that his mind is well-informed, enjoyment of books exceedingly great, his imagination lively, his observation just and correct, and his taste delicate and pure. His abilities in every respect improve as much upon acquaintance as his manners and person. At first sight, his address is certainly not striking; and his person can hardly be called handsome, till the expression of his eyes, which are uncommonly good, and the general sweetness of his countenance, is perceived. At present, I know him so well, that I think him really handsome; or at least, almost so. What say you, Marianne?"

"I shall very soon think him handsome, Elinor, if I do not now. When you tell me to love him as a brother, I shall no more see imperfection in his face, than I now do in his heart."

Elinor started at this declaration, and was sorry for the warmth she had been betrayed into, in speaking of him. She felt that Edward stood very high in her opinion. She believed the regard to be mutual; but she required greater certainty of it to make Marianne's conviction of their attachment agreeable to her. She knew that what Marianne and her mother conjectured one moment, they believed the next – that with them, to wish was to hope, and to hope was to expect. She tried to explain the real state of the case to her sister.

"I do not attempt to deny," said she, "that I think very highly of him – that I greatly esteem, that I like him."

Marianne here burst forth with indignation –

"Esteem him! Like him! Cold-hearted Elinor! Oh! worse than cold-hearted! Ashamed of being otherwise. Use those words again, and I will leave the room this moment."

Elinor could not help laughing. "Excuse me," said she; "and be assured that I meant no offence to you, by speaking, in so quiet a way, of my own feelings. Believe them to be stronger than I have declared; believe them, in short, to be such as his merit, and the suspicion – the hope of his affection for me may warrant, without imprudence or folly. But farther than this you must not believe. I am by no means assured of his regard for me. There are moments when the extent of it seems doubtful; and till his sentiments are fully known, you cannot wonder at my wishing to avoid any encouragement of my own partiality, by believing or calling it more than it is. In my heart I feel little – scarcely any doubt of his preference. But there are other points to be considered besides his inclination. He is very far from being independent. What his mother really is we cannot know; but, from Fanny's occasional mention of her conduct and opinions, we have never been disposed to think her amiable; and I am very much mistaken if Edward is not himself aware that there would be many difficulties in his way, if he were to wish to marry a woman who had not either a great fortune or high rank."

Marianne was astonished to find how much the imagination of her mother and herself had outstripped the truth.

"And you really are not engaged to him!" said she. "Yet it certainly soon will happen. But two advantages will proceed from this delay. I shall not lose you so soon, and Edward will have greater opportunity of improving that natural taste for your favourite pursuit which must be so indispensably necessary to your future felicity. Oh! if he should be so far stimulated by your genius as to learn to draw himself, how delightful it would be!"

Elinor had given her real opinion to her sister. She could not consider her partiality for Edward in so prosperous a state as Marianne had believed it. There was, at times, a want of spirits about him which, if it did not denote indifference, spoke of something almost as unpromising. A doubt of her regard, supposing him to feel it, need not give him more than inquietude. It would not be likely to produce that dejection of mind which frequently attended him. A more reasonable cause might be found in the dependent situation which forbade the indulgence of his affection. She knew that his mother neither behaved to him so as to make his home comfortable at present, nor to give him any assurance that he might form a home for himself, without strictly attending to her views for his aggrandizement. With such a knowledge as this, it was impossible for Elinor to feel easy on the subject. She was far from depending on that result of his preference of her, which her mother and sister still considered as certain. Nay, the longer they were together the more doubtful seemed the nature of his regard; and sometimes, for a few painful minutes, she believed it to be no more than friendship.

But, whatever might really be its limits, it was enough, when perceived by his sister, to make her uneasy, and at the same time, (which was still more common,) to make her uncivil. She took the first opportunity of affronting her mother-in-law on the occasion, talking to her so expressively of her brother's great expectations, of Mrs. Ferrars's resolution that both her sons should marry well, and of the danger attending any young woman who attempted to **draw him in**; that Mrs. Dashwood could neither pretend to be unconscious, nor endeavor to be calm. She gave her an answer which marked her contempt, and instantly left the room, resolving that, whatever might be the inconvenience or expense of so sudden a removal, her beloved Elinor should not be exposed another week to such insinuations.

In this state of her spirits, a letter was delivered to her from the post, which contained a proposal particularly well timed. It was the offer of a small house, on very easy terms, belonging to a relation of her own, a gentleman of consequence and property in Devonshire. The letter was from this gentleman himself, and written in the true spirit of friendly accommodation. He understood that she was in need of a dwelling; and though the house he now offered her was merely a cottage, he assured her that everything should be done to it which she might think necessary, if the situation pleased her. He earnestly pressed her, after giving the particulars of the house and garden, to come with her daughters to Barton Park, the place of his own residence, from whence she might judge, herself, whether Barton Cottage, for the houses were in the same parish, could, by any alteration, be made comfortable to her. He seemed really anxious to accommodate them and the whole of his letter was written in so friendly a style as could not fail of giving pleasure to his cousin; more especially at a moment when she was suffering under the cold and unfeeling behaviour of her nearer connections. She needed no time for deliberation or inquiry. Her resolution was formed as she read. The situation of Barton, in a county so far distant from Sussex as Devonshire, which, but a few hours before, would have been a sufficient objection to outweigh every possible advantage belonging to the place, was now its first recommendation. To quit the neighbourhood of Norland was no longer an evil; it was an object of desire; it was a blessing, in comparison of the misery of continuing her daughter-in-law's guest; and to remove for ever from that beloved place would be less painful than to inhabit or visit it while such a woman was its mistress. She instantly wrote Sir John Middleton her acknowledgment of his kindness, and her acceptance of his proposal; and then hastened to shew both letters to her daughters, that she might be secure of their approbation before her answer were sent.

Elinor had always thought it would be more prudent for them to settle at some distance from Norland, than immediately amongst their present acquaintance. On **that** head, therefore, it was not for her to oppose her mother's intention of removing into Devonshire. The house, too, as described by Sir John, was on so simple a scale, and the rent so uncommonly moderate, as to leave her no right of objection on either point; and, therefore, though it was not a plan which brought any charm to her fancy, though it was a removal from the vicinity of Norland beyond her wishes, she made no attempt to dissuade her mother from sending a letter of acquiescence.

CHAPTER FIVE

NO SOONER was her answer dispatched, than Mrs. Dashwood indulged herself in the pleasure of announcing to her son-in-law and his wife that she was provided with a house, and should incommode them no longer than till every thing were ready for her inhabiting it. They heard her with surprise. Mrs. John Dashwood said nothing; but her husband civilly hoped that she would not be settled far from Norland. She had great satisfaction in replying that she was going into Devonshire. – Edward turned hastily towards her, on hearing this, and, in a voice of surprise and concern, which required no explanation to her, repeated, "Devonshire! Are you, indeed, going there? So far from hence! And to what part of it?" She explained the situation. It was within four miles northward of Exeter.

"It is but a cottage," she continued, "but I hope to see many of my friends in it. A room or two can easily be added; and if my friends find no difficulty in travelling so far to see me, I am sure I will find none in accommodating them."

She concluded with a very kind invitation to Mr. and Mrs. John Dashwood to visit her at Barton; and to Edward she gave one with still greater affection. Though her late conversation with her daughter-in-law had made her resolve on remaining at Norland no longer than was unavoidable, it had not produced the smallest effect on her in that point to which it principally tended.

To separate Edward and Elinor was as far from being her object as ever; and she wished to show Mrs. John Dashwood, by this pointed invitation to her brother, how totally she disregarded her disapprobation of the match.

Mr. John Dashwood told his mother again and again how exceedingly sorry he was that she had taken a house at such a distance from Norland as to prevent his being of any service to her in removing her furniture. He really felt conscientiously vexed on the occasion; for the very exertion to which he had limited the performance of his promise to his father was by this arrangement rendered impracticable. – The furniture was all sent around by water. It chiefly consisted of household linen, plate, china, and books, with a handsome pianoforte of Marianne's. Mrs. John Dashwood saw the packages depart with a sigh: she could not help feeling it hard that as Mrs. Dashwood's income would be so trifling in comparison with their own, she should have any handsome article of furniture.

Mrs. Dashwood took the house for a twelvemonth; it was ready furnished, and she might have immediate possession. No difficulty arose on either side in the agreement; and she waited only for the disposal of her effects at Norland, and to determine her future household, before she set off for the west; and this, as she was exceedingly rapid in the performance of everything that interested her, was soon done. – The horses which were left her by her husband had been sold soon after his death, and an opportunity now offering of disposing of her carriage, she agreed to sell that likewise at the earnest advice of her eldest daughter. For the comfort of her children, had she consulted only her own wishes, she would have kept it; but the discretion of Elinor prevailed. **her** wisdom too limited the number of their servants to three; two maids and a man, with whom they were speedily provided from amongst those who had formed their establishment at Norland.

The man and one of the maids were sent off immediately into Devonshire, to prepare the house for their mistress's arrival; for as Lady Middleton was entirely unknown to Mrs. Dashwood, she preferred going directly to the cottage to being a visitor at Barton Park; and she relied so undoubtingly on Sir John's description of the house, as to feel no curiosity to examine it herself till she entered it as her own. Her eagerness to be gone from Norland was preserved from diminution by the evident satisfaction of her daughter-in-law in the prospect of her removal; a satisfaction which was but feebly attempted to be concealed under a cold invitation to her to defer her departure. Now was the time when her son-in-law's promise to his father might with particular propriety be fulfilled. Since he had neglected to do it on first coming to the estate, their quitting his house might be looked on as the most suitable period for its accomplishment. But Mrs. Dashwood began shortly to give over every hope of the kind, and to be convinced, from the general drift of his discourse, that his assistance extended no farther than their maintenance for six months at Norland. He so frequently talked of the increasing expenses of housekeeping, and of the perpetual demands upon his purse, which a man of any consequence in the world was beyond calculation exposed to, that he seemed rather to stand in need of more money himself than to have any design of giving money away.

In a very few weeks from the day which brought Sir John Middleton's first letter to Norland, every thing was so far settled in their future abode as to enable Mrs. Dashwood and her daughters to begin their journey.

Many were the tears shed by them in their

last adieus to a place so much beloved. "Dear, dear Norland!" said Marianne, as she wandered alone before the house, on the last evening of their being there; "when shall I cease to regret you! – when learn to feel a home elsewhere! – Oh! happy house, could you know what I suffer in now viewing you from this spot, from whence perhaps I may view you no more! – And you, ye well-known trees! – but you will continue the same. – No leaf will decay because we are removed, nor any branch become motionless although we can observe you no longer! – No; you will continue the same; unconscious of the pleasure or the regret you occasion, and insensible of any change in those who walk under your shade! – But who will remain to enjoy you?"

CHAPTER SIX

THE FIRST PART of their journey was performed in too melancholy a disposition to be otherwise than tedious and unpleasant. But as they drew towards the end of it, their interest in the appearance of a country which they were to inhabit overcame their dejection, and a view of Barton Valley as they entered it gave them cheerfulness. It was a pleasant fertile spot, well wooded, and rich in pasture. After winding along it for more than a mile, they reached their own house. A small green court was the whole of its demesne in front; and a neat wicket gate admitted them into it.

As a house, Barton Cottage, though small, was comfortable and compact; but as a cottage it was defective, for the building was regular, the roof was tiled, the window shutters were not painted green, nor were the walls covered with honeysuckles. A narrow passage led directly through the house into the garden behind. On each side of the entrance was a sitting room, about sixteen feet square; and beyond them were the offices and the stairs. Four bedrooms and two garrets formed the rest of the house. It had not been built many years and was in good repair. In comparison of Norland, it was poor and small indeed! – but the tears which recollection called forth as they entered the house were soon dried away. They were cheered by the joy of the servants on their arrival, and each for the sake of the others resolved to appear happy.

Chapter Six

It was very early in September; the season was fine, and from first seeing the place under the advantage of good weather, they received an impression in its favour which was of material service in recommending it to their lasting approbation.

The situation of the house was good. High hills rose immediately behind, and at no great distance on each side; some of which were open downs, the others cultivated and woody. The village of Barton was chiefly on one of these hills, and formed a pleasant view from the cottage windows. The prospect in front was more extensive; it commanded the whole of the valley, and reached into the country beyond. The hills which surrounded the cottage terminated the valley in that direction; under another name, and in another course, it branched out again between two of the steepest of them.

With the size and furniture of the house Mrs. Dashwood was upon the whole well satisfied; for though her former style of life rendered many additions to the latter indispensable, yet to add and improve was a delight to her; and she had at this time ready money enough to supply all that was wanted of greater elegance to the apartments. “As for the house itself, to be sure,” said she, “it is too small for our family, but we will make ourselves tolerably comfortable for the present, as it is too late in the year for improvements. Perhaps in the spring, if I have plenty of money, as I dare say I shall, we may think about building. These parlors are both too small for such parties of our friends as I hope to see often collected here; and I have some thoughts of throwing the passage into one of them with perhaps a part of the other, and so leave the remainder of that other for an entrance; this, with a new drawing room which may be easily added, and a bed-chamber and garret above, will make it a very snug little cottage. I could wish the stairs were handsome. But one must not expect every thing; though I suppose it would be no difficult matter to widen them. I shall see how much I am before-hand with the world in the spring, and we will plan our improvements accordingly."

In the mean time, till all these alterations could be made from the savings of an income of five hundred a-year by a woman who never saved in her life, they were wise enough to be contented with the house as it was; and each of them was busy in arranging their particular concerns, and endeavoring, by placing around them books and other possessions, to form themselves a home. Marianne's pianoforte was unpacked and properly disposed of; and Elinor's drawings were affixed to the walls of their sitting room.

In such employments as these they were interrupted soon after breakfast the next day by the entrance of their landlord, who called to welcome them to Barton, and to offer them every accommodation from his own house and garden in which theirs might at present be deficient. Sir John Middleton was a good looking man about forty. He had formerly visited at Stanhill, but it was too long for his young cousins to remember him. His countenance was thoroughly good-humoured; and his manners were as friendly as the style of his letter. Their arrival seemed to afford him real satisfaction, and their comfort to be an object of real solicitude to him. He said much of his earnest desire of their living in the most sociable terms with his family, and pressed them so cordially to dine at Barton Park every day till they were better settled at home, that, though his entreaties were carried to a point of perseverance beyond civility, they could not give offence. His kindness was not confined to words; for within an hour after he left them, a large basket full of garden stuff and fruit arrived from the park, which was followed before the end of the day by a present of game. He insisted, moreover, on conveying all their letters to and from the post for them, and would not be denied the satisfaction of sending them his newspaper every day.

Lady Middleton had sent a very civil message by him, denoting her intention of waiting on Mrs. Dashwood as soon as she could be assured that her visit would be no inconvenience; and as this message was answered by an invitation equally polite, her ladyship was introduced to them the next day.

They were, of course, very anxious to see a person on whom so much of their comfort at Barton must depend; and the elegance of her appearance was favourable to their wishes. Lady Middleton was not more than six or seven and twenty; her face was handsome, her figure tall and striking, and her address graceful. Her manners had all the elegance which her husband's wanted. But they would have been improved by some share of his frankness and warmth; and her visit was long enough to detract something from their first admiration, by shewing that, though perfectly well-bred, she was reserved, cold, and had nothing to say for herself beyond the most common-place inquiry or remark.

Conversation however was not wanted, for Sir John was very chatty, and Lady Middleton had taken the wise precaution of bringing with her their eldest child, a fine little boy about six years old, by which means there was one subject always to be recurred to by the ladies in case of extremity, for they had to enquire his name and age, admire his beauty, and ask him questions which his mother answered for him, while he hung about her and held down his head, to the great surprise of her ladyship, who wondered at his being so shy before company, as he could make noise enough at home. On every formal visit a child ought to be of the party, by way of provision for discourse. In the present case it took up ten minutes to determine whether the boy were most like his father or mother, and in what particular he resembled either, for of course every body differed, and every body was astonished at the opinion of the others.

An opportunity was soon to be given to the Dashwoods of debating on the rest of the children, as Sir John would not leave the house without securing their promise of dining at the park the next day.

CHAPTER SEVEN

BARTON PARK was about half a mile from the cottage. The ladies had passed near it in their way along the valley, but it was screened from their view at home by the projection of a hill. The house was large and handsome; and the Middletons lived in a style of equal hospitality and elegance. The former was for Sir John's gratification, the latter for that of his lady. They were scarcely ever without some friends staying with them in the house, and they kept more company of every kind than any other family in the neighbourhood. It was necessary to the happiness of both; for however dissimilar in temper and outward behaviour, they strongly resembled each other in that total want of talent and taste which confined their employments, unconnected with such as society produced, within a very narrow compass. Sir John was a sportsman, Lady Middleton a mother. He hunted and shot, and she humoured her children; and these were their only resources. Lady Middleton had the advantage of being able to spoil her children all the year round, while Sir John's independent employments were in existence only half the time. Continual engagements at home and abroad, however, supplied all the deficiencies of nature and education; supported the good spirits of Sir John, and gave exercise to the good breeding of his wife.

Lady Middleton piqued herself upon the elegance of her table, and of all her domestic arrangements; and from this kind of vanity was her greatest enjoyment in any of their parties. But Sir John's satisfaction in society was much more real; he delighted in collecting about him more young people than his house would hold, and the noisier they were the better was he pleased. He was a blessing to all the juvenile part of the neighbourhood, for in summer he was for ever forming parties to eat cold ham and chicken out of doors, and in winter his private balls were numerous enough for any young lady who was not suffering under the unsatiable appetite of fifteen.

The arrival of a new family in the country was always a matter of joy to him, and in every point of view he was charmed with the inhabitants he had now procured for his cottage at Barton. The Miss Dashwoods were young, pretty, and unaffected. It was enough to secure his good opinion; for to be unaffected was all that a pretty girl could want to make her mind as captivating as her person. The friendliness of his disposition made him happy in accommodating those, whose situation might be considered, in comparison with the past, as unfortunate. In showing kindness to his cousins therefore he had the real satisfaction of a good heart; and in settling a family of females only in his cottage, he had all the satisfaction of a sportsman; for a sportsman, though he esteems only those of his sex who are sportsmen likewise, is not often desirous of encouraging their taste by admitting them to a residence within his own manor.

Mrs. Dashwood and her daughters were met at the door of the house by Sir John, who welcomed them to Barton Park with unaffected sincerity; and as he attended them to the drawing room repeated to the young ladies the concern which the same subject had drawn from him the day before, at being unable to get any smart young men to meet them. They would see, he said, only one gentleman there besides himself;

a particular friend who was staying at the park, but who was neither very young nor very gay. He hoped they would all excuse the smallness of the party, and could assure them it should never happen so again. He had been to several families that morning in hopes of procuring some addition to their number, but it was moonlight and every body was full of engagements. Luckily Lady Middleton's mother had arrived at Barton within the last hour, and as she was a very cheerful agreeable woman, he hoped the young ladies would not find it so very dull as they might imagine. The young ladies, as well as their mother, were perfectly satisfied with having two entire strangers of the party, and wished for no more.

Mrs. Jennings, Lady Middleton's mother, was a good-humoured, merry, fat, elderly woman, who talked a great deal, seemed very happy, and rather vulgar. She was full of jokes and laughter, and before dinner was over had said many witty things on the subject of lovers and husbands; hoped they had not left their hearts behind them in Sussex, and pretended to see them blush whether they did or not. Marianne was vexed at it for her sister's sake, and turned her eyes towards Elinor to see how she bore these attacks, with an earnestness which gave Elinor far more pain than could arise from such common-place raillery as Mrs. Jennings's.

Colonel Brandon, the friend of Sir John, seemed no more adapted by resemblance of manner to be his friend, than Lady Middleton was to be his wife, or Mrs. Jennings to be Lady Middleton's mother. He was silent and grave. His appearance however was not unpleasing, in spite of his being in the opinion of Marianne and Margaret an absolute old bachelor, for he was on the wrong side of five and thirty; but though his face was not handsome, his countenance was sensible, and his address was particularly gentlemanlike.

There was nothing in any of the party which could recommend them as companions to the Dashwoods; but the cold insipidity of Lady Middleton was so particularly repulsive, that in comparison of it the gravity of Colonel Brandon, and even the boisterous mirth of Sir John and his mother-in-law was interesting. Lady Middleton seemed to be roused to enjoyment only by the entrance of her four noisy children after dinner, who pulled her about, tore her clothes, and put an end to every kind of discourse except what related to themselves.

In the evening, as Marianne was discovered to be musical, she was invited to play. The instrument was unlocked, every body prepared to be charmed, and Marianne, who sang very well, at their request went through the chief of the songs which Lady Middleton had brought into the family on her marriage, and which perhaps had lain ever since in the same position on the pianoforte, for her ladyship had celebrated that event by giving up music, although by her mother's account, she had played extremely well, and by her own was very fond of it.

Marianne's performance was highly applauded. Sir John was loud in his admiration at the end of every song, and as loud in his conversation with the others while every song lasted. Lady Middleton frequently called him to order, wondered how any one's attention could be diverted from music for a moment, and asked Marianne to sing a particular song which Marianne had just finished. Colonel Brandon alone, of all the party, heard her without being in raptures. He paid her only the compliment of attention; and she felt a respect for him on the occasion, which the others had reasonably forfeited by their shameless want of taste. His pleasure in music, though it amounted not to that ecstatic delight which alone could sympathize with her own, was estimable when contrasted against the horrible insensibility of the others; and she was reasonable enough to allow that a man of five and thirty might well have outlived all acuteness of feeling and every exquisite power of enjoyment. She was perfectly disposed to make every allowance for the colonel's advanced state of life which humanity required.

CHAPTER EIGHT

MRS. JENNINGS was a widow with an ample jointure. She had only two daughters, both of whom she had lived to see respectably married, and she had now therefore nothing to do but to marry all the rest of the world. In the promotion of this object she was zealously active, as far as her ability reached; and missed no opportunity of projecting weddings among all the young people of her acquaintance. She was remarkably quick in the discovery of attachments, and had enjoyed the advantage of raising the blushes and the vanity of many a young lady by insinuations of her power over such a young man; and this kind of discernment enabled her soon after her arrival at Barton decisively to pronounce that Colonel Brandon was very much in love with Marianne Dashwood. She rather suspected it to be so, on the very first evening of their being together, from his listening so attentively while she sang to them; and when the visit was returned by the Middletons' dining at the cottage, the fact was ascertained by his listening to her again. It must be so. She was perfectly convinced of it. It would be an excellent match, for **he** was rich, and **she** was handsome. Mrs. Jennings had been anxious to see Colonel Brandon well married, ever since her connection with Sir John first brought him to her knowledge; and she was always anxious to get a good husband for every pretty girl.

The immediate advantage to herself was by no means inconsiderable, for it supplied her with endless jokes against them both. At the park she laughed at the colonel, and in the cottage at Marianne. To the former her raillery was probably, as far as it regarded only himself, perfectly indifferent; but to the latter it was at first incomprehensible; and when its object was understood, she hardly knew whether most to laugh at its absurdity, or censure its impertinence, for she considered it as an unfeeling reflection on the colonel's advanced years, and on his forlorn condition as an old bachelor.

Mrs. Dashwood, who could not think a man five years younger than herself, so exceedingly ancient as he appeared to the youthful fancy of her daughter, ventured to clear Mrs. Jennings from the probability of wishing to throw ridicule on his age.

"But at least, Mama, you cannot deny the absurdity of the accusation, though you may not think it intentionally ill-natured. Colonel

Brandon is certainly younger than Mrs. Jennings, but he is old enough to be **my** father; and if he were ever animated enough to be in love, must have long outlived every sensation of the kind. It is too ridiculous! When is a man to be safe from such wit, if age and infirmity will not protect him?"

"Infirmity!" said Elinor, "do you call Colonel Brandon infirm? I can easily suppose that his age may appear much greater to you than to my mother; but you can hardly deceive yourself as to his having the use of his limbs!"

"Did not you hear him complain of the rheumatism? and is not that the commonest infirmity of declining life?"

"My dearest child," said her mother, laughing, "at this rate you must be in continual terror of **my** decay; and it must seem to you a miracle that my life has been extended to the advanced age of forty."

"Mama, you are not doing me justice. I know very well that Colonel Brandon is not old enough to make his friends yet apprehensive of losing him in the course of nature. He may live twenty years longer. But thirty-five has nothing to do with matrimony."

"Perhaps," said Elinor, "thirty-five and seventeen had better not have any thing to do with matrimony together. But if there should by any chance happen to be a woman who is single at seven and twenty, I should not think Colonel Brandon's being thirty-five any objection to his marrying **her**."

"A woman of seven and twenty," said Marianne, after pausing a moment, "can never hope to feel or inspire affection again, and if her home be uncomfortable, or her fortune small, I can suppose that she might bring herself to submit to the offices of a nurse, for the sake of the provision and security of a wife. In his marrying such a woman therefore there would be nothing unsuitable. It would be a compact of convenience, and the world would be satisfied. In my eyes it would be no marriage at all, but that would be nothing. To me it would seem only a commercial exchange, in which each wished to be benefited at the expense of the other."

"It would be impossible, I know," replied Elinor, "to convince you that a woman of seven and twenty could feel for a man of thirty-five anything near enough to love, to make him a desirable companion to her. But I must object to your dooming Colonel Brandon and his wife to the constant confinement of a sick chamber, merely because he chanced to complain yesterday (a very cold damp day) of a slight rheumatic feel in one of his shoulders."

"But he talked of flannel waistcoats," said Marianne; "and with me a flannel waistcoat is invariably connected with aches, cramps, rheumatisms, and every species of ailment that can afflict the old and the feeble."

"Had he been only in a violent fever, you would not have despised him half so much. Confess, Marianne, is not there something interesting to you in the flushed cheek, hollow eye, and quick pulse of a fever?"

Soon after this, upon Elinor's leaving the room, "Mama," said Marianne, "I have an alarm on the subject of illness which I cannot conceal from you. I am sure Edward Ferrars is not well. We have now been here almost a fortnight, and yet he does not come. Nothing but real indisposition could occasion this extraordinary delay. What else can detain him at Norland?"

"Had you any idea of his coming so soon?" said Mrs. Dashwood. "I had none. On the contrary, if I have felt any anxiety at all on the subject, it has been in recollecting that he sometimes showed a want of pleasure and readiness in accepting my invitation, when I talked of his coming to Barton. Does Elinor expect him already?"

"I have never mentioned it to her, but of course she must."

"I rather think you are mistaken, for when I was talking to her yesterday of getting a new grate for the spare bedchamber, she observed that there was no immediate hurry for it, as it was not likely that the room would be wanted for some time."

"How strange this is! what can be the meaning of it! But the whole of their behaviour to each other has been unaccountable! How cold, how composed were their last adieus! How languid their conversation the last evening of their being together! In Edward's farewell there was no distinction between Elinor and me: it was the good wishes of an affectionate brother to both. Twice did I leave them purposely together in the course of the last morning, and each time did he most unaccountably follow me out of the room. And Elinor, in quitting Norland and Edward, cried not as I did. Even now her self-command is invariable. When is she dejected or melancholy? When does she try to avoid society, or appear restless and dissatisfied in it?"

CHAPTER NINE

THE DASHWOODS were now settled at Barton with tolerable comfort to themselves. The house and the garden, with all the objects surrounding them, were now become familiar, and the ordinary pursuits which had given to Norland half its charms were engaged in again with far greater enjoyment than Norland had been able to afford, since the loss of their father. Sir John Middleton, who called on them every day for the first fortnight, and who was not in the habit of seeing much occupation at home, could not conceal his amazement on finding them always employed.

Their visitors, except those from Barton Park, were not many; for, in spite of Sir John's urgent entreaties that they would mix more in the neighbourhood, and repeated assurances of his carriage being always at their service, the independence of Mrs. Dashwood's spirit overcame the wish of society for her children; and she was resolute in declining to visit any family beyond the distance of a walk. There were but few who could be so classed; and it was not all of them that were attainable. About a mile and a half from the cottage, along the narrow winding valley of Allenham, which issued from that of Barton, as formerly described, the girls had, in one of their earliest walks, discovered an ancient respectable looking mansion which, by reminding them a little of Norland, interested their imagination and made them wish to be better acquainted with it. But they learnt, on enquiry, that its possessor, an elderly lady of very good character, was unfortunately too infirm to mix with the world, and never stirred from home.

The whole country about them abounded in beautiful walks. The high downs which invited them from almost every window of the cottage to seek the exquisite enjoyment of air on their summits, were a happy alternative when the dirt of the valleys beneath shut up their superior beauties; and towards one of these hills did Marianne and Margaret one memorable morning direct their steps, attracted by the partial sunshine of a showery sky, and unable longer to bear the confinement which the settled rain of the two preceding days had occasioned. The weather was not tempting enough to draw the two others from their pencil and their book, in spite of Marianne's declaration that the day would be lastingly fair, and that every threatening cloud would be drawn off from their hills; and the two girls set off together.

They gaily ascended the downs, rejoicing in their own penetration at every glimpse of blue sky; and when they caught in their faces the animating gales of a high south-westerly wind, they pitied the fears which had prevented their mother and Elinor from sharing such delightful sensations.

"Is there a felicity in the world," said Marianne, "superior to this? – Margaret, we will walk here at least two hours."

Margaret agreed, and they pursued their way against the wind, resisting it with laughing delight for about twenty minutes longer, when suddenly the clouds united over their heads, and a driving rain set full in their face. – Chagrined and surprised, they were obliged, though unwillingly, to turn back, for no shelter was nearer than their own house. One consolation however remained for them, to which the exigence of the moment gave more than usual propriety;

it was that of running with all possible speed down the steep side of the hill which led immediately to their garden gate.

They set off. Marianne had at first the advantage, but a false step brought her suddenly to the ground; and Margaret, unable to stop herself to assist her, was involuntarily hurried along, and reached the bottom in safety.

A gentleman carrying a gun, with two pointers playing round him, was passing up the hill and within a few yards of Marianne, when her accident happened. He put down his gun and ran to her assistance. She had raised herself from the ground, but her foot had been twisted in her fall, and she was scarcely able to stand. The gentleman offered his services; and perceiving that her modesty declined what her situation rendered necessary, took her up in his arms without farther delay, and carried her down the hill. Then passing through the garden, the gate of which had been left open by

Margaret, he bore her directly into the house, whither Margaret was just arrived, and quitted not his hold till he had seated her in a chair in the parlour.

Elinor and her mother rose up in amazement at their entrance, and while the eyes of both were fixed on him with an evident wonder and a secret admiration which equally sprung from his appearance, he apologized for his intrusion by relating its cause, in a manner so frank and so graceful that his person, which was uncommonly handsome, received additional charms from his voice and expression. Had he been even old, ugly, and vulgar, the gratitude and kindness of Mrs. Dashwood would have been secured by any act of attention to her child; but the influence of youth, beauty, and elegance, gave an interest to the action which came home to her feelings.

She thanked him again and again; and, with a sweetness of address which always attended her, invited him to be seated. But this he declined, as he was dirty and wet. Mrs. Dashwood then begged to know to whom she was obliged. His name, he replied, was Willoughby, and his present home was at Allenham, from whence he hoped she would allow him the honour of calling tomorrow to enquire after Miss Dashwood. The honour was readily granted, and he then departed, to make himself still more interesting, in the midst of a heavy rain.

His manly beauty and more than common gracefulness were instantly the theme of general admiration, and the laugh which his gallantry raised against Marianne received particular spirit from his exterior attractions. – Marianne herself had seen less of his person than the rest, for the confusion which crimsoned over her face, on his lifting her up, had robbed her of the power of regarding him after their entering the house. But she had seen enough of him to join in all the admiration of the others, and with an energy which always adorned her praise. His person and air were equal to what her fancy had ever drawn for the hero of a favourite story; and in his carrying her into the house with so little previous formality, there was a rapidity of thought which particularly recommended the action to her. Every circumstance belonging to him was interesting. His name was good, his residence was in their favourite village, and she soon found out that of all manly dresses a shooting-jacket was the most becoming. Her imagination was busy, her reflections were pleasant, and the pain of a sprained ankle was disregarded.

Sir John called on them as soon as the next interval of fair weather that morning allowed him to get out of doors; and Marianne's accident being related to him, he was eagerly asked whether he knew any gentleman of the name of Willoughby at Allenham.

"Willoughby!" cried Sir John; "what, is **he** in the country? That is good news however;

I will ride over tomorrow, and ask him to dinner on Thursday."

"You know him then," said Mrs. Dashwood.

"Know him! to be sure I do. Why, he is down here every year."

"And what sort of a young man is he?"

"As good a kind of fellow as ever lived, I assure you. A very decent shot, and there is not a bolder rider in England."

"And is that all you can say for him?" cried Marianne, indignantly. "But what are his manners on more intimate acquaintance? What his pursuits, his talents, and genius?"

Sir John was rather puzzled.

"Upon my soul," said he, "I do not know much about him as to all **that**. But he is a pleasant, good humoured fellow, and has got the nicest little black bitch of a pointer I ever saw. Was she out with him today?"

But Marianne could no more satisfy him as to the colour of Mr. Willoughby's pointer, than he could describe to her the shades of his mind.

"But who is he?" said Elinor. "Where does he come from? Has he a house at Allenham?"

On this point Sir John could give more certain intelligence; and he told them that Mr. Willoughby had no property of his own in the country; that he resided there only while he was visiting the old lady at Allenham Court, to whom he was related, and whose possessions he was to inherit; adding, "Yes, yes, he is very well worth catching I can tell you, Miss Dashwood; he has a pretty little estate of his own in Somersetshire besides; and if I were you, I would not give him up to my younger sister, in spite of all this tumbling down hills. Miss Marianne must not expect to have all the men to herself. Brandon will be jealous, if she does not take care."

"I do not believe," said Mrs. Dashwood, with a good humoured smile, "that Mr. Willoughby will be incommoded by the attempts of either of **my** daughters towards what you call **catching** him. It is not an employment to which they have been brought up. Men are very safe with us, let them be ever so rich. I am glad to find, however, from what you say, that he is a respectable young man, and one whose acquaintance will not be ineligible."

"He is as good a sort of fellow, I believe, as ever lived," repeated Sir John. "I remember last Christmas at a little hop at the park, he danced from eight o'clock till four, without once sitting down."

"Did he indeed?" cried Marianne with sparkling eyes, "and with elegance, with spirit?"

"Yes; and he was up again at eight to ride to covert."

"That is what I like; that is what a young man ought to be. Whatever be his pursuits, his eagerness in them should know no moderation, and leave him no sense of fatigue."

"Aye, aye, I see how it will be," said Sir John, "I see how it will be. You will be setting your cap at him now, and never think of poor Brandon."

"That is an expression, Sir John," said Marianne, warmly, "which I particularly dislike. I abhor every common-place phrase by which wit is intended; and 'setting one's cap at a man,' or 'making a conquest,' are the most odious of all. Their tendency is gross and illiberal; and if their construction could ever be deemed clever, time has long ago destroyed all its ingenuity."

Sir John did not much understand this reproof; but he laughed as heartily as if he did, and then replied,

"Ay, you will make conquests enough, I dare say, one way or other. Poor Brandon! he is quite smitten already, and he is very well worth setting your cap at, I can tell you, in spite of all this tumbling about and spraining of ankles."

CHAPTER TEN

MARIANNE'S PRESERVER, as Margaret, with more elegance than precision, styled Willoughby, called at the cottage early the next morning to make his personal enquiries. He was received by Mrs. Dashwood with more than politeness; with a kindness which Sir John's account of him and her own gratitude prompted; and every thing that passed during the visit tended to assure him of the sense, elegance, mutual affection, and domestic comfort of the family to whom accident had now introduced him. Of their personal charms he had not required a second interview to be convinced.

Miss Dashwood had a delicate complexion, regular features, and a remarkably pretty figure. Marianne was still handsomer. Her form, though not so correct as her sister's, in having the advantage of height, was more striking; and her face was so lovely, that when in the common cant of praise, she was called a beautiful girl, truth was less violently outraged than usually happens. Her skin was very brown, but, from its transparency, her complexion was uncommonly brilliant; her features were all good; her smile was sweet and attractive; and in her eyes, which were very dark, there was a life, a spirit, an eagerness, which could hardily be seen without delight. From Willoughby their expression was at first held back, by the embarrassment which the remembrance of his assistance created. But when this passed away, when her spirits became collected, when she saw that to the perfect good-breeding of the gentleman, he united frankness and vivacity, and above all, when she heard him declare, that of music and dancing he was passionately fond, she gave him such a look of approbation as secured the largest share of his discourse to herself for the rest of his stay.

It was only necessary to mention any favourite amusement to engage her to talk. She could not be silent when such points were introduced, and she had neither shyness nor reserve in their discussion. They speedily discovered that their enjoyment of dancing and music was mutual, and that it arose from a general conformity of judgment in all that related to either. Encouraged by this to a further examination of his opinions, she proceeded to question him on the subject of books; her favourite authors were brought forward and dwelt upon with so rapturous a delight, that any young man of five and twenty must have been insensible indeed, not to become an immediate convert to the excellence of such works, however disregarded before. Their taste was strikingly alike. The same books, the same passages were idolized by each – or if any difference appeared, any objection arose, it lasted no longer than till the force of her arguments and the brightness of her eyes could be displayed. He acquiesced in all her decisions, caught all her enthusiasm; and long before his visit concluded, they conversed with the familiarity of a long-established acquaintance.

"Well, Marianne," said Elinor, as soon as he had left them, "for **one** morning I think you have done pretty well. You have already ascertained Mr. Willoughby's opinion in almost every matter of importance. You know what he thinks of Cowper and Scott; you are certain of his estimating their beauties as he ought, and you have received every assurance of his admiring Pope no more than is proper. But how is your acquaintance to be long supported, under such extraordinary despatch of every subject for discourse? You will soon have exhausted each favourite topic. Another meeting will suffice to explain his sentiments on picturesque beauty, and second marriages, and then you can have nothing farther to ask." –

"Elinor," cried Marianne, "is this fair? is this just? are my ideas so scanty? But I see what you mean. I have been too much at my ease, too happy, too frank. I have erred against every common-place notion of decorum; I have been open and sincere where I ought to have been reserved, spiritless, dull, and deceitful – had I talked only of the weather and the roads, and had I spoken only once in ten minutes, this reproach would have been spared."

"My love," said her mother, "you must not be offended with Elinor – she was only in jest. I should scold her myself, if she were capable of wishing to check the delight of your conversation with our new friend." – Marianne was softened in a moment.

Willoughby, on his side, gave every proof of his pleasure in their acquaintance, which an evident wish of improving it could offer. He came to them every day. To enquire after Marianne was at first his excuse; but the encouragement of his reception, to which every day gave greater kindness, made such an excuse unnecessary before it had ceased to be possible, by Marianne's perfect recovery. She was confined for some days to the house; but never had any confinement been less irksome. Willoughby was a young man of good abilities, quick imagination, lively spirits, and open, affectionate manners. He was exactly formed to engage Marianne's heart, for with all this, he joined not only a captivating person, but a natural ardour of mind which was now roused and increased by the example of her own, and which recommended him to her affection beyond every thing else.

His society became gradually her most exquisite enjoyment. They read, they talked, they sang together; his musical talents were considerable; and he read with all the sensibility and spirit which Edward had unfortunately wanted.

In Mrs. Dashwood's estimation he was as faultless as in Marianne's; and Elinor saw nothing to censure in him but a propensity, in which he strongly resembled and peculiarly delighted her sister, of saying too much what he thought on every occasion, without attention to persons or circumstances. In hastily forming and giving his opinion of other people, in sacrificing general politeness to the enjoyment of undivided attention where his heart was engaged, and in slighting too easily the forms of worldly propriety, he displayed a want of caution which Elinor could not approve, in spite of all that he and Marianne could say in its support.

Marianne began now to perceive that the

desperation which had seized her at sixteen and a half, of ever seeing a man who could satisfy her ideas of perfection, had been rash and unjustifiable. Willoughby was all that her fancy had delineated in that unhappy hour and in every brighter period, as capable of attaching her; and his behaviour declared his wishes to be in that respect as earnest, as his abilities were strong.

Her mother too, in whose mind not one speculative thought of their marriage had been raised, by his prospect of riches, was led before the end of a week to hope and expect it; and secretly to congratulate herself on having gained two such sons-in-law as Edward and Willoughby.

Colonel Brandon's partiality for Marianne, which had so early been discovered by his friends, now first became perceptible to Elinor, when it ceased to be noticed by them. Their attention and wit were drawn off to his more fortunate rival; and the raillery which the other had incurred before any partiality arose, was removed when his feelings began really to call for the ridicule so justly annexed to sensibility. Elinor was obliged, though unwillingly, to believe that the sentiments which Mrs. Jennings had assigned him for her own satisfaction, were now actually excited by her sister; and that however a general resemblance of disposition between the parties might forward the affection of Mr. Willoughby, an equally striking opposition of character was no hindrance to the regard of Colonel Brandon. She saw it with concern; for what could a silent man of five and thirty hope, when opposed to a very lively one of five and twenty? and as she could not even wish him successful, she heartily wished him indifferent. She liked him – in spite of his gravity and reserve, she beheld in him an object of interest. His manners, though serious, were mild; and his reserve appeared rather the result of some oppression of spirits than of any natural gloominess of temper. Sir

John had dropped hints of past injuries and disappointments, which justified her belief of his being an unfortunate man, and she regarded him with respect and compassion.

Perhaps she pitied and esteemed him the more because he was slighted by Willoughby and Marianne, who, prejudiced against him for being neither lively nor young, seemed resolved to undervalue his merits.

"Brandon is just the kind of man," said Willoughby one day, when they were talking of him together, "whom every body speaks well of, and nobody cares about; whom all are delighted to see, and nobody remembers to talk to."

"That is exactly what I think of him," cried Marianne.

"Do not boast of it, however," said Elinor, "for it is injustice in both of you. He is highly esteemed by all the family at the park, and I never see him myself without taking pains to converse with him."

"That he is patronised by **you**," replied

Willoughby, "is certainly in his favour; but as for the esteem of the others, it is a reproach in itself. Who would submit to the indignity of being approved by such a woman as Lady Middleton and Mrs. Jennings, that could command the indifference of any body else?"

"But perhaps the abuse of such people as yourself and Marianne will make amends for the regard of Lady Middleton and her mother. If their praise is censure, your censure may be praise, for they are not more undiscerning, than you are prejudiced and unjust."

"In defence of your protege you can even be saucy."

"My protege, as you call him, is a sensible man; and sense will always have attractions for me. Yes, Marianne, even in a man between thirty and forty. He has seen a great deal of the world; has been abroad, has read, and has a thinking mind. I have found him capable of giving me much information on various subjects; and he has always answered my inquiries with readiness of good-breeding and good nature."

"That is to say," cried Marianne contemptuously, "he has told you, that in the East Indies the climate is hot, and the mosquitoes are troublesome."

"He **would** have told me so, I doubt not, had I made any such inquiries, but they happened to be points on which I had been previously informed."

"Perhaps," said Willoughby, "his observations may have extended to the existence of nabobs, gold mohrs, and palanquins."

"I may venture to say that **his** observations have stretched much further than your candour. But why should you dislike him?"

"I do not dislike him. I consider him, on the contrary, as a very respectable man, who has every body's good word, and nobody's notice; who, has more money than he can spend, more time than he knows how to employ, and two new coats every year."

"Add to which," cried Marianne, "that he has neither genius, taste, nor spirit. That his understanding has no brilliancy, his feelings no ardour, and his voice no expression."

"You decide on his imperfections so much in the mass," replied Elinor, "and so much on the strength of your own imagination, that the commendation I am able to give of him is comparatively cold and insipid. I can only pronounce him to be a sensible man, well-bred, well-informed, of gentle address, and, I believe, possessing an amiable heart."

"Miss Dashwood," cried Willoughby, "you are now using me unkindly. You are endeavouring to disarm me by reason, and to convince me against my will. But it will not do. You shall find me as stubborn as you can be artful. I have three unanswerable reasons for disliking Colonel Brandon; he threatened me with rain when I wanted it to be fine; he has found fault with the hanging of my curricle, and I cannot persuade him to buy my brown mare. If it will be any satisfaction to you, however, to be told, that I believe his character to be in other respects irreproachable, I am ready to confess it. And in return for an acknowledgment, which must give me some pain, you cannot deny me the privilege of disliking him as much as ever."

CHAPTER ELEVEN

LITTLE HAD MRS. DASHWOOD or her daughters imagined when they first came into Devonshire, that so many engagements would arise to occupy their time as shortly presented themselves, or that they should have such frequent invitations and such constant visitors as to leave them little leisure for serious employment. Yet such was the case. When Marianne was recovered, the schemes of amusement at home and abroad, which

Sir John had been previously forming, were put into execution. The private balls at the park then began; and parties on the water were made and accomplished as often as a showery October would allow. In every meeting of the kind Willoughby was included; and the ease and familiarity which naturally attended these parties were exactly calculated to give increasing intimacy to his acquaintance with the Dashwoods, to afford him opportunity of witnessing the excellencies of Marianne, of marking his animated admiration of her, and of receiving, in her behaviour to himself, the most pointed assurance of her affection.

Elinor could not be surprised at their attachment. She only wished that it were less openly shewn; and once or twice did venture to suggest the propriety of some self-command to Marianne. But Marianne abhorred all concealment where no real disgrace could attend unreserve; and to aim at the restraint of sentiments which were not in themselves illaudable, appeared to her not merely an unnecessary effort, but a disgraceful subjection of reason to common-place and mistaken notions. Willoughby thought the same; and their behaviour at all times, was an illustration of their opinions.

When he was present she had no eyes for any one else. Every thing he did, was right. Every thing he said, was clever. If their evenings at the park were concluded with cards, he cheated himself and all the rest of the party to get her a good hand. If dancing formed the amusement of the night, they were partners for half the time; and when obliged to separate for a couple of dances, were careful to stand together and scarcely spoke a word to any body else. Such conduct made them of course most exceedingly laughed at; but ridicule could not shame, and seemed hardly to provoke them.

Mrs. Dashwood entered into all their feelings

with a warmth which left her no inclination for checking this excessive display of them. To her it was but the natural consequence of a strong affection in a young and ardent mind.

This was the season of happiness to Marianne. Her heart was devoted to Willoughby, and the fond attachment to Norland, which she brought with her from Sussex, was more likely to be softened than she had thought it possible before, by the charms which his society bestowed on her present home.

Elinor's happiness was not so great. Her heart was not so much at ease, nor her satisfaction in their amusements so pure. They afforded her no companion that could make amends for what she had left behind, nor that could teach her to think of Norland with less regret than ever. Neither Lady Middleton nor Mrs. Jennings could supply to her the conversation she missed; although the latter was an everlasting talker, and from the first had regarded her with a kindness which ensured her a large share of her discourse. She had already repeated her own history to Elinor three or four times; and had Elinor's memory been equal to her means of improvement, she might have known very early in their acquaintance all the particulars of Mr. Jennings's last illness, and what he said to his wife a few minutes before he died. Lady Middleton was more agreeable than her mother only in being more silent. Elinor needed little observation to perceive that her reserve was a mere calmness of manner with which sense had nothing to do. Towards her husband and mother she was the same as to them; and intimacy was therefore neither to be looked for nor desired. She had nothing to say one day that she had not said the day before. Her insipidity was invariable, for even her spirits were always the same; and though she did not oppose the parties arranged by her husband, provided every thing were conducted in style and her two eldest children attended her, she never appeared to receive more enjoyment from them than she might have experienced in sitting at home; – and so little did her presence add to the pleasure of the others, by any share in their conversation, that they were sometimes only reminded of her being amongst them by her solicitude about her troublesome boys.

In Colonel Brandon alone, of all her new acquaintance, did Elinor find a person who could in any degree claim the respect of abilities, excite the interest of friendship, or give pleasure as a companion. Willoughby was out of the question. Her admiration and regard, even her sisterly regard, was all his own; but he was a lover; his attentions were wholly Marianne's, and a far less agreeable man might have been more generally pleasing. Colonel Brandon, unfortunately for himself, had no such encouragement to think only of Marianne, and in conversing with Elinor he found the greatest consolation for the indifference of her sister.

Elinor's compassion for him increased, as she had reason to suspect that the misery of disappointed love had already been known to him. This suspicion was given by some words which accidentally dropped from him one evening at the park, when they were sitting down together by mutual consent, while the others were dancing. His eyes were fixed on Marianne, and, after a silence of some minutes, he said, with a faint smile, "Your sister, I understand, does not approve of second attachments."

"No," replied Elinor, "her opinions are all romantic."

"Or rather, as I believe, she considers them impossible to exist."

"I believe she does. But how she contrives it without reflecting on the character of her own father, who had himself two wives, I know not. A few years however will settle her opinions on the reasonable basis of common sense and observation; and then they may be more easy to define and to justify than they now are, by any body but herself."

"This will probably be the case," he replied; "and yet there is something so amiable in the prejudices of a young mind, that one is sorry to see them give way to the reception of more general opinions."

"I cannot agree with you there," said Elinor. "There are inconveniences attending such feelings as Marianne's, which all the charms of enthusiasm and ignorance of the world cannot atone for. Her systems have all the unfortunate tendency of setting propriety at nought; and a better acquaintance with the world is what I look forward to as her greatest possible advantage."

After a short pause he resumed the conversation by saying, –

"Does your sister make no distinction in her objections against a second attachment?

or is it equally criminal in every body? Are those who have been disappointed in their first choice, whether from the inconstancy of its object, or the perverseness of circumstances, to be equally indifferent during the rest of their lives?"

"Upon my word, I am not acquainted with the minutiae of her principles. I only know that I never yet heard her admit any instance of a second attachment's being pardonable."

"This," said he, "cannot hold; but a change, a total change of sentiments – No, no, do not desire it; for when the romantic refinements of a young mind are obliged to give way, how frequently are they succeeded by such opinions as are but too common, and too dangerous! I speak from experience. I once knew a lady who in temper and mind greatly resembled your sister, who thought and judged like her, but who from an inforced change – from a series of unfortunate circumstances" – Here he stopt suddenly;

appeared to think that he had said too much, and by his countenance gave rise to conjectures, which might not otherwise have entered Elinor's head. The lady would probably have passed without suspicion, had he not convinced Miss Dashwood that what concerned her ought not to escape his lips. As it was, it required but a slight effort of fancy to connect his emotion with the tender recollection of past regard. Elinor attempted no more. But Marianne, in her place, would not have done so little. The whole story would have been speedily formed under her active imagination; and every thing established in the most melancholy order of disastrous love.

CHAPTER TWELVE

AS ELINOR AND MARIANNE were walking together the next morning the latter communicated a piece of news to her sister, which in spite of all that she knew before of Marianne's imprudence and want of thought, surprised her by its extravagant testimony of both. Marianne told her, with the greatest delight, that Willoughby had given her a horse, one that he had bred himself on his estate in Somersetshire, and which was exactly calculated to carry a woman.

Without considering that it was not in her mother's plan to keep any horse, that if she were to alter her resolution in favour of this gift, she must buy another for the servant, and keep a servant to ride it, and after all, build a stable to receive them, she had accepted the present without hesitation, and told her sister of it in raptures.

"He intends to send his groom into Somersetshire immediately for it," she added, "and when it arrives we will ride every day. You shall share its use with me. Imagine to yourself, my dear Elinor, the delight of a gallop on some of these downs."

Most unwilling was she to awaken from such a dream of felicity to comprehend all the unhappy truths which attended the affair; and for some time she refused to submit to them. As to an additional servant, the expense would be a trifle; Mama she was sure would never object to it; and any horse would do for **him**; he might always get one at the park; as to a stable, the merest shed would be sufficient. Elinor then ventured to doubt the propriety of her receiving such a present from a man so little, or at least so lately known to her. This was too much.

"You are mistaken, Elinor," said she warmly, "in supposing I know very little of Willoughby. I have not known him long indeed, but I am much better acquainted with him, than I am with any other creature in the world, except yourself and mama. It is not time or opportunity that is to determine intimacy; – it is disposition alone. Seven years would be insufficient to make some people acquainted with each other, and seven days are more than enough for others. I should hold myself guilty of greater impropriety in accepting a horse from my brother, than from Willoughby. Of John I know very little, though we have lived together for years; but of Willoughby my judgment has long been formed."

Elinor thought it wisest to touch that point no more. She knew her sister's temper.

Opposition on so tender a subject would only attach her the more to her own opinion. But by an appeal to her affection for her mother, by representing the inconveniences which that indulgent mother must draw on herself, if (as would probably be the case) she consented to this increase of establishment, Marianne was shortly subdued; and she promised not to tempt her mother to such imprudent kindness by mentioning the offer, and to tell Willoughby when she saw him next, that it must be declined.

She was faithful to her word; and when Willoughby called at the cottage, the same day, Elinor heard her express her disappointment to him in a low voice, on being obliged to forego the acceptance of his present. The reasons for this alteration were at the same time related, and they were such as to make further entreaty on his side impossible. His concern however was very apparent; and after expressing it with earnestness, he added, in the same low voice, – "But, Marianne, the horse is still yours, though you cannot use it now. I shall keep it only till you can claim it. When you leave Barton to form your own establishment in a more lasting home, Queen Mab shall receive you."

This was all overheard by Miss Dashwood; and in the whole of the sentence, in his manner of pronouncing it, and in his addressing her sister by her Christian name alone, she instantly saw an intimacy so decided, a meaning so direct, as marked a perfect agreement between them. From that moment she doubted not of their being engaged to each other; and the belief of it created no other surprise than that she, or any of their friends, should be left by tempers so frank, to discover it by accident.

Margaret related something to her the next day, which placed this matter in a still clearer light. Willoughby had spent the preceding evening with them, and Margaret, by being left some time in the parlour with only him and Marianne, had had opportunity for observations, which, with a most important face, she communicated to her eldest sister, when they were next by themselves.

"Oh, Elinor!" she cried, "I have such a secret to tell you about Marianne. I am sure she will be married to Mr. Willoughby very soon."

"You have said so," replied Elinor, "almost every day since they first met on High-church Down; and they had not known each other a week, I believe, before you were certain that Marianne wore his picture round her neck; but it turned out to be only the miniature of our great uncle."

"But indeed this is quite another thing. I am sure they will be married very soon, for he has got a lock of her hair."

"Take care, Margaret. It may be only the hair of some great uncle of **his**."

"But, indeed, Elinor, it is Marianne's. I am almost sure it is, for I saw him cut it off. Last night after tea, when you and mama went out of the room, they were whispering and talking together as fast as could be, and he seemed to be begging something of her, and presently he took up her scissors and cut off a long lock of her hair, for it was all tumbled down her back; and he kissed it, and folded it up in a piece of white paper; and put it into his pocket-book."

For such particulars, stated on such authority, Elinor could not withhold her credit; nor was she disposed to it, for the circumstance was in perfect unison with what she had heard and seen herself.

Margaret's sagacity was not always displayed in a way so satisfactory to her sister. When Mrs. Jennings attacked her one evening at the park, to give the name of the young man who was Elinor's particular favourite, which had been long a matter of great curiosity to her, Margaret answered by looking at her sister, and saying, "I must not tell, may I, Elinor?"

This of course made every body laugh; and

Elinor tried to laugh too. But the effort was painful. She was convinced that Margaret had fixed on a person whose name she could not bear with composure to become a standing joke with Mrs. Jennings.

Marianne felt for her most sincerely; but she did more harm than good to the cause, by turning very red and saying in an angry manner to Margaret,

"Remember that whatever your conjectures may be, you have no right to repeat them."

"I never had any conjectures about it," replied Margaret; "it was you who told me of it yourself."

This increased the mirth of the company, and Margaret was eagerly pressed to say something more.

"Oh! pray, Miss Margaret, let us know all about it," said Mrs. Jennings. "What is the gentleman's name?"

"I must not tell, ma'am. But I know very well what it is; and I know where he is too."

"Yes, yes, we can guess where he is; at

his own house at Norland to be sure. He is the curate of the parish I dare say."

"No, **that** he is not. He is of no profession at all."

"Margaret," said Marianne with great warmth, "you know that all this is an invention of your own, and that there is no such person in existence."

"Well, then, he is lately dead, Marianne, for I am sure there was such a man once, and his name begins with an F."

Most grateful did Elinor feel to Lady Middleton for observing, at this moment, "that it rained very hard," though she believed the interruption to proceed less from any attention to her, than from her ladyship's great dislike of all such inelegant subjects of raillery as delighted her husband and mother. The idea however started by her, was immediately pursued by Colonel Brandon, who was on every occasion mindful of the feelings of others; and much was said on the subject of rain by both of them. Willoughby opened the piano-forte, and asked Marianne to sit down to it; and thus amidst the various endeavours of different people to quit the topic, it fell to the ground. But not so easily did Elinor recover from the alarm into which it had thrown her.

A party was formed this evening for going on the following day to see a very fine place about twelve miles from Barton, belonging to a brother-in-law of Colonel Brandon, without whose interest it could not be seen, as the proprietor, who was then abroad, had left strict orders on that head. The grounds were declared to be highly beautiful, and Sir John, who was particularly warm in their praise, might be allowed to be a tolerable judge, for he had formed parties to visit them, at least, twice every summer for the last ten years. They contained a noble piece of water; a sail on which was to a form a great part of the morning's amusement; cold provisions were to be taken, open carriages only to be employed, and every thing conducted in the usual style of a complete party of pleasure.

To some few of the company it appeared rather a bold undertaking, considering the time of year, and that it had rained every day for the last fortnight; – and Mrs. Dashwood, who had already a cold, was persuaded by Elinor to stay at home.

CHAPTER THIRTEEN

THEIR INTENDED EXCURSION to Whitwell turned out very different from what Elinor had expected. She was prepared to be wet through, fatigued, and frightened; but the event was still more unfortunate, for they did not go at all.

By ten o'clock the whole party was assembled at the park, where they were to breakfast. The morning was rather favourable, though it had rained all night, as the clouds were then dispersing across the sky, and the sun frequently appeared. They were all in high spirits and good humour, eager to be happy, and determined to submit to the greatest inconveniences and hardships rather than be otherwise.

While they were at breakfast the letters were brought in. Among the rest there was one for Colonel Brandon; – he took it, looked at the direction, changed colour, and immediately left the room.

"What is the matter with Brandon?" said Sir John.

Nobody could tell.

"I hope he has had no bad news," said Lady Middleton. "It must be something extraordinary that could make Colonel Brandon leave my breakfast table so suddenly."

In about five minutes he returned.

"No bad news, Colonel, I hope;" said Mrs. Jennings, as soon as he entered the room.

"None at all, ma'am, I thank you."

"Was it from Avignon? I hope it is not to

say that your sister is worse."

"No, ma'am. It came from town, and is merely a letter of business."

"But how came the hand to discompose you so much, if it was only a letter of business? Come, come, this won't do, Colonel; so let us hear the truth of it."

"My dear madam," said Lady Middleton, "recollect what you are saying."

"Perhaps it is to tell you that your cousin Fanny is married?" said Mrs. Jennings, without attending to her daughter's reproof.

"No, indeed, it is not."

"Well, then, I know who it is from, Colonel. And I hope she is well."

"Whom do you mean, ma'am?" said he, colouring a little.

"Oh! you know who I mean."

"I am particularly sorry, ma'am," said he, addressing Lady Middleton, "that I should receive this letter today, for it is on business which requires my immediate attendance in town."

"In town!" cried Mrs. Jennings. "What can you have to do in town at this time of year?"

"My own loss is great," he continued, "in being obliged to leave so agreeable a party; but I am the more concerned, as I fear my presence is necessary to gain your admittance at Whitwell."

What a blow upon them all was this!

"But if you write a note to the housekeeper, Mr. Brandon," said Marianne, eagerly, "will it not be sufficient?"

He shook his head.

"We must go," said Sir John. – "It shall not be put off when we are so near it. You cannot go to town till tomorrow, Brandon, that is all."

"I wish it could be so easily settled. But it is not in my power to delay my journey for one day!"

"If you would but let us know what your business is," said Mrs. Jennings, "we might see whether it could be put off or not."

"You would not be six hours later," said

Willoughby, "if you were to defer your journey till our return."

"I cannot afford to lose **one** hour." –

Elinor then heard Willoughby say, in a low voice to Marianne, "There are some people who cannot bear a party of pleasure. Brandon is one of them. He was afraid of catching cold I dare say, and invented this trick for getting out of it. I would lay fifty guineas the letter was of his own writing."

"I have no doubt of it," replied Marianne.

"There is no persuading you to change your mind, Brandon, I know of old," said Sir John, "when once you are determined on anything. But, however, I hope you will think better of it. Consider, here are the two Miss Careys come over from Newton, the three Miss Dashwoods walked up from the cottage, and Mr. Willoughby got up two hours before his usual time, on purpose to go to Whitwell."

Colonel Brandon again repeated his sorrow at being the cause of disappointing the party; but at the same time declared it to be unavoidable.

"Well, then, when will you come back again?"

"I hope we shall see you at Barton," added her ladyship, "as soon as you can conveniently leave town; and we must put off the party to Whitwell till you return."

"You are very obliging. But it is so uncertain, when I may have it in my power to return, that I dare not engage for it at all."

"Oh! he must and shall come back," cried Sir John. "If he is not here by the end of the week, I shall go after him."

"Ay, so do, Sir John," cried Mrs. Jennings, "and then perhaps you may find out what his business is."

"I do not want to pry into other men's concerns. I suppose it is something he is ashamed of."

Colonel Brandon's horses were announced.

"You do not go to town on horseback, do you?" added Sir John.

"No. Only to Honiton. I shall then go post."

"Well, as you are resolved to go, I wish you a good journey. But you had better change your mind."

"I assure you it is not in my power."

He then took leave of the whole party.

"Is there no chance of my seeing you and your sisters in town this winter, Miss Dashwood?"

"I am afraid, none at all."

"Then I must bid you farewell for a longer time than I should wish to do."

To Marianne, he merely bowed and said nothing.

"Come Colonel," said Mrs. Jennings, "before you go, do let us know what you are going about."

He wished her a good morning, and, attended by Sir John, left the room.

The complaints and lamentations which politeness had hitherto restrained, now burst forth universally; and they all agreed again and again how provoking it was to be so disappointed.

"I can guess what his business is, however," said Mrs. Jennings exultingly.

"Can you, ma'am?" said almost every body.

"Yes; it is about Miss Williams, I am sure."

"And who is Miss Williams?" asked Marianne.

"What! do not you know who Miss Williams is? I am sure you must have heard of her before. She is a relation of the Colonel's, my dear; a very near relation. We will not say how near, for fear of shocking the young ladies." Then, lowering her voice a little, she said to Elinor, "She is his natural daughter."

"Indeed!"

"Oh, yes; and as like him as she can stare. I dare say the Colonel will leave her all his fortune."

When Sir John returned, he joined most heartily in the general regret on so unfortunate an event; concluding however by observing, that as they were all got together, they must do something by way of being happy; and after some consultation it was agreed, that although happiness could only be enjoyed at Whitwell, they might procure a tolerable composure of mind by driving about the country. The carriages were then ordered; Willoughby's was first, and Marianne never looked happier than when she got into it. He drove through the park very fast, and they were soon out of sight; and nothing more of them was seen till their return, which did not happen till after the return of all the rest. They both seemed delighted with their drive; but said only in general terms that they had kept in the lanes, while the others went on the downs.

It was settled that there should be a dance in the evening, and that every body should be extremely merry all day long. Some more of the Careys came to dinner, and they had the pleasure of sitting down nearly twenty to table, which Sir John observed with great contentment. Willoughby took his usual place between the two elder Miss Dashwoods. Mrs. Jennings sat on Elinor's right hand; and they had not been long seated, before she leant behind her and Willoughby, and said to Marianne, loud enough for them both to hear, "I have found you out in spite of all your tricks. I know where you spent the morning."

Marianne coloured, and replied very hastily, "Where, pray?" –

"Did not you know," said Willoughby, "that we had been out in my curricle?"

"Yes, yes, Mr. Impudence, I know that very well, and I was determined to find out **where** you had been to. – I hope you like your house, Miss Marianne. It is a very large one, I know; and when I come to see you, I hope you will have new-furnished it, for it wanted it very much when I was there six years ago."

Marianne turned away in great confusion. Mrs. Jennings laughed heartily; and Elinor found that in her resolution to know where they had been, she had actually made her own woman enquire of Mr. Willoughby's groom; and that she had by that method been informed that they had gone to Allenham, and spent a considerable time there in walking about the garden and going all over the house.

Elinor could hardly believe this to be true, as it seemed very unlikely that Willoughby should propose, or Marianne consent, to enter the house while Mrs. Smith was in it, with whom Marianne had not the smallest acquaintance.

As soon as they left the dining-room, Elinor enquired of her about it; and great was her surprise when she found that every circumstance related by Mrs. Jennings was perfectly true. Marianne was quite angry with her for doubting it.

"Why should you imagine, Elinor, that we did not go there, or that we did not see the house? Is not it what you have often wished to do yourself?"

"Yes, Marianne, but I would not go while Mrs. Smith was there, and with no other companion than Mr. Willoughby."

"Mr. Willoughby however is the only person who can have a right to shew that house; and as he went in an open carriage, it was impossible to have any other companion. I never spent a pleasanter morning in my life."

"I am afraid," replied Elinor, "that the pleasantness of an employment does not always evince its propriety."

"On the contrary, nothing can be a stronger proof of it, Elinor; for if there had been any real impropriety in what I did, I should have been sensible of it at the time, for we always know when we are acting wrong, and with such a conviction I could have had no pleasure."

"But, my dear Marianne, as it has already exposed you to some very impertinent remarks, do you not now begin to doubt the discretion of your own conduct?"

"If the impertinent remarks of Mrs. Jennings are to be the proof of impropriety in conduct, we are all offending every moment of our lives. I value not her censure any more than I should do her commendation. I am not sensible of having done anything wrong in walking over Mrs. Smith's grounds, or in seeing her house. They will one day be Mr. Willoughby's, and – "

"If they were one day to be your own, Marianne, you would not be justified in what you have done."

She blushed at this hint; but it was even visibly gratifying to her; and after a ten minutes' interval of earnest thought, she came to her sister again, and said with great good humour, "Perhaps, Elinor, it **was** rather ill-judged in me to go to Allenham; but Mr. Willoughby wanted particularly to shew me the place; and it is a charming house, I assure you. – There is one remarkably pretty sitting room up stairs; of a nice comfortable size for constant use, and with modern furniture it would be delightful. It is a corner room, and has windows on two sides. On one side you look across the bowling-green, behind the house, to a beautiful hanging wood, and on the other you have a view of the church and village, and, beyond them, of those fine bold hills that we have so often admired. I did not see it to advantage, for nothing could be more forlorn than the furniture, – but if it were newly fitted up – a couple of hundred pounds, Willoughby says, would make it one of the pleasantest summer-rooms in England."

Could Elinor have listened to her without interruption from the others, she would have described every room in the house with equal delight.

CHAPTER FOURTEEN

THE SUDDEN TERMINATION of Colonel Brandon's visit at the park, with his steadiness in concealing its cause, filled the mind, and raised the wonder of Mrs. Jennings for two or three days; she was a great wonderer, as every one must be who takes a very lively interest in all the comings and goings of all their acquaintance. She wondered, with little intermission what could be the reason of it; was sure there must be some bad news, and thought over every kind of distress that could have befallen him, with a fixed determination that he should not escape them all.

"Something very melancholy must be the matter, I am sure," said she. "I could see it in his face. Poor man! I am afraid his circumstances may be bad. The estate at Delaford was never reckoned more than two thousand a year, and his brother left everything sadly involved. I do think he must have been sent for about money matters, for what else can it be? I wonder whether it is so. I would give anything to know the truth of it. Perhaps it is about Miss Williams and, by the bye, I dare say it is, because he looked so conscious when I mentioned her. May be she is ill in town; nothing in the world more likely, for I have a notion she is always rather sickly. I would lay any wager it is about Miss Williams. It is not so very likely he should be distressed in his circumstances **now**, for he is a very prudent man, and to be sure must have cleared the estate by this time. I wonder what it can be!

May be his sister is worse at Avignon, and has sent for him over. His setting off in such a hurry seems very like it. Well, I wish him out of all his trouble with all my heart, and a good wife into the bargain."

So wondered, so talked Mrs. Jennings. Her opinion varying with every fresh conjecture, and all seeming equally probable as they arose. Elinor, though she felt really interested in the welfare of Colonel Brandon, could not bestow all the wonder on his going so suddenly away, which Mrs. Jennings was desirous of her feeling; for besides that the circumstance did not in her opinion justify such lasting amazement or variety of speculation, her wonder was otherwise disposed of. It was engrossed by the extraordinary silence of her sister and Willoughby on the subject, which they must know to be peculiarly interesting to them all. As this silence continued, every day made it appear more strange and more incompatible with the disposition of both.

Why they should not openly acknowledge to her mother and herself, what their constant behaviour to each other declared to have taken place, Elinor could not imagine.

She could easily conceive that marriage might not be immediately in their power; for though Willoughby was independent, there was no reason to believe him rich. His estate had been rated by Sir John at about six or seven hundred a year; but he lived at an expense to which that income could hardly be equal, and he had himself often complained of his poverty. But for this strange kind of secrecy maintained by them relative to their engagement, which in fact concealed nothing at all, she could not account; and it was so wholly contradictory to their general opinions and practice, that a doubt sometimes entered her mind of their being really engaged, and this doubt was enough to prevent her making any inquiry of Marianne.

Nothing could be more expressive of

attachment to them all, than Willoughby's behaviour. To Marianne it had all the distinguishing tenderness which a lover's heart could give, and to the rest of the family it was the affectionate attention of a son and a brother. The cottage seemed to be considered and loved by him as his home; many more of his hours were spent there than at Allenham; and if no general engagement collected them at the park, the exercise which called him out in the morning was almost certain of ending there, where the rest of the day was spent by himself at the side of Marianne, and by his favourite pointer at her feet.

One evening in particular, about a week after Colonel Brandon left the country, his heart seemed more than usually open to every feeling of attachment to the objects around him; and on Mrs. Dashwood's happening to mention her design of improving the cottage in the spring, he warmly opposed every alteration of a place which affection had established as perfect with him.

"What!" he exclaimed – "Improve this dear cottage! No. **that** I will never consent to. Not a stone must be added to its walls, not an inch to its size, if my feelings are regarded."

"Do not be alarmed," said Miss Dashwood, "nothing of the kind will be done; for my mother will never have money enough to attempt it."

"I am heartily glad of it," he cried. "May she always be poor, if she can employ her riches no better."

"Thank you, Willoughby. But you may be assured that I would not sacrifice one sentiment of local attachment of yours, or of any one whom I loved, for all the improvements in the world. Depend upon it that whatever unemployed sum may remain, when I make up my accounts in the spring, I would even rather lay it uselessly by than dispose of it in a manner so painful to you. But are you really so attached to this place as to see no defect in it?"

"I am," said he. "To me it is faultless. Nay, more, I consider it as the only form of building in which happiness is attainable, and were I rich enough I would instantly pull Combe down, and build it up again in the exact plan of this cottage."

"With dark narrow stairs and a kitchen that smokes, I suppose," said Elinor.

"Yes," cried he in the same eager tone, "with all and every thing belonging to it; – in no one convenience or **in**convenience about it, should the least variation be perceptible. Then, and then only, under such a roof, I might perhaps be as happy at Combe as I have been at Barton."

"I flatter myself," replied Elinor, "that even under the disadvantage of better rooms and a broader staircase, you will hereafter find your own house as faultless as you now do this."

"There certainly are circumstances," said Willoughby, "which might greatly endear it to me; but this place will always have one claim of my affection, which no other can possibly share."

Mrs. Dashwood looked with pleasure at Marianne, whose fine eyes were fixed so expressively on Willoughby, as plainly denoted how well she understood him.

"How often did I wish," added he, "when I was at Allenham this time twelvemonth, that Barton cottage were inhabited! I never passed within view of it without admiring its situation, and grieving that no one should live in it. How little did I then think that the very first news I should hear from Mrs. Smith, when I next came into the country, would be that Barton cottage was taken: and I felt an immediate satisfaction and interest in the event, which nothing but a kind of prescience of what happiness I should experience from it, can account for. Must it not have been so, Marianne?" speaking to her in a lowered voice. Then continuing his former tone, he said, "And yet this house you would spoil,

Mrs. Dashwood? You would rob it of its simplicity by imaginary improvement! and this dear parlour in which our acquaintance first began, and in which so many happy hours have been since spent by us together, you would degrade to the condition of a common entrance, and every body would be eager to pass through the room which has hitherto contained within itself more real accommodation and comfort than any other apartment of the handsomest dimensions in the world could possibly afford."

Mrs. Dashwood again assured him that no alteration of the kind should be attempted.

"You are a good woman," he warmly replied. "Your promise makes me easy. Extend it a little farther, and it will make me happy. Tell me that not only your house will remain the same, but that I shall ever find you and yours as unchanged as your dwelling; and that you will always consider me with the kindness which has made everything belonging to you so dear to me."

The promise was readily given, and Willoughby's behaviour during the whole of the evening declared at once his affection and happiness.

"Shall we see you tomorrow to dinner?" said Mrs. Dashwood, when he was leaving them. "I do not ask you to come in the morning, for we must walk to the park, to call on Lady Middleton."

He engaged to be with them by four o'clock.

CHAPTER FIFTEEN

MRS. DASHWOOD'S VISIT to Lady Middleton took place the next day, and two of her daughters went with her; but Marianne excused herself from being of the party, under some trifling pretext of employment; and her mother, who concluded that a promise had been made by Willoughby the night before of calling on her while they were absent, was perfectly satisfied with her remaining at home.

On their return from the park they found

Willoughby's curricle and servant in waiting at the cottage, and Mrs. Dashwood was convinced that her conjecture had been just. So far it was all as she had foreseen; but on entering the house she beheld what no foresight had taught her to expect. They were no sooner in the passage than Marianne came hastily out of the parlour apparently in violent affliction, with her handkerchief at her eyes; and without noticing them ran up stairs. Surprised and alarmed they proceeded directly into the room she had just quitted, where they found only Willoughby, who was leaning against the mantel-piece with his back towards them. He turned round on their coming in, and his countenance shewed that he strongly partook of the emotion which overpowered Marianne.

"Is anything the matter with her?" cried Mrs. Dashwood as she entered – "is she ill?"

"I hope not," he replied, trying to look

cheerful; and with a forced smile presently added, "It is I who may rather expect to be ill – for I am now suffering under a very heavy disappointment!"

"Disappointment?"

"Yes, for I am unable to keep my engagement with you. Mrs. Smith has this morning exercised the privilege of riches upon a poor dependent cousin, by sending me on business to London. I have just received my dispatches, and taken my farewell of Allenham; and by way of exhilaration I am now come to take my farewell of you."

"To London! – and are you going this morning?"

"Almost this moment."

"This is very unfortunate. But Mrs. Smith must be obliged; – and her business will not detain you from us long I hope."

He coloured as he replied, "You are very kind, but I have no idea of returning into Devonshire immediately. My visits to Mrs. Smith are never repeated within the twelvemonth."

"And is Mrs. Smith your only friend? Is Allenham the only house in the neighbourhood to which you will be welcome? For shame, Willoughby, can you wait for an invitation here?"

His colour increased; and with his eyes fixed on the ground he only replied, "You are too good."

Mrs. Dashwood looked at Elinor with surprise. Elinor felt equal amazement. For a few moments every one was silent. Mrs. Dashwood first spoke.

"I have only to add, my dear Willoughby, that at Barton cottage you will always be welcome; for I will not press you to return here immediately, because you only can judge how far **that** might be pleasing to Mrs. Smith; and on this head I shall be no more disposed to question your judgment than to doubt your inclination."

"My engagements at present," replied Willoughby, confusedly, "are of such a nature – that – I dare not flatter myself" –

He stopt. Mrs. Dashwood was too much astonished to speak, and another pause succeeded. This was broken by Willoughby, who said with a faint smile, "It is folly to linger in this manner. I will not torment myself any longer by remaining among friends whose society it is impossible for me now to enjoy."

He then hastily took leave of them all and left the room. They saw him step into his carriage, and in a minute it was out of sight.

Mrs. Dashwood felt too much for speech, and instantly quitted the parlour to give way in solitude to the concern and alarm which this sudden departure occasioned.

Elinor's uneasiness was at least equal to her mother's. She thought of what had just passed with anxiety and distrust. Willoughby's behaviour in taking leave of them, his embarrassment, and affectation of cheerfulness, and, above all, his unwillingness to accept her mother's invitation, a backwardness so unlike a lover, so unlike himself, greatly disturbed her. One moment she feared that no serious design had ever been formed on his side; and the next that some unfortunate quarrel had taken place between him and her sister; – the distress in which Marianne had quitted the room was such as a serious quarrel could most reasonably account for, though when she considered what Marianne's love for him was, a quarrel seemed almost impossible.

But whatever might be the particulars of their separation, her sister's affliction was indubitable; and she thought with the tenderest compassion of that violent sorrow which Marianne was in all probability not merely giving way to as a relief, but feeding and encouraging as a duty.

In about half an hour her mother returned, and though her eyes were red, her countenance was not uncheerful.

"Our dear Willoughby is now some miles from Barton, Elinor," said she, as she sat down to work, “and with how heavy a heart does he travel?”

“It is all very strange. So suddenly to be gone! It seems but the work of a moment. And last night he was with us so happy, so cheerful, so affectionate? And now, after only ten minutes notice – Gone too without intending to return! – Something more than what he owned to us must have happened. He did not speak, he did not behave like himself. **you** must have seen the difference as well as I. What can it be? Can they have quarrelled? Why else should he have shewn such unwillingness to accept your invitation here?” –

“It was not inclination that he wanted, Elinor; I could plainly see **that**. He had not the power of accepting it. I have thought it all over I assure you, and I can perfectly account for every thing that at first seemed strange to me as well as to you.”

“Can you, indeed!”

“Yes. I have explained it to myself in the

most satisfactory way; – but you, Elinor, who love to doubt where you can – it will not satisfy **you**, I know; but you shall not talk **me** out of my trust in it. I am persuaded that Mrs. Smith suspects his regard for Marianne, disapproves of it, (perhaps because she has other views for him,) and on that account is eager to get him away; – and that the business which she sends him off to transact is invented as an excuse to dismiss him. This is what I believe to have happened. He is, moreover, aware that she **does** disapprove the connection, he dares not therefore at present confess to her his engagement with Marianne, and he feels himself obliged, from his dependent situation, to give into her schemes, and absent himself from Devonshire for a while. You will tell me, I know, that this may or may **not** have happened; but I will listen to no cavil, unless you can point out any other method of understanding the affair as satisfactory at this. And now, Elinor, what have you to say?”

“Nothing, for you have anticipated my answer.”

“Then you would have told me, that it might or might not have happened. Oh, Elinor, how incomprehensible are your feelings! You had rather take evil upon credit than good. You had rather look out for misery for Marianne, and guilt for poor Willoughby, than an apology for the latter. You are resolved to think him blameable, because he took leave of us with less affection than his usual behaviour has shewn. And is no allowance to be made for inadvertence, or for spirits depressed by recent disappointment? Are no probabilities to be accepted, merely because they are not certainties? Is nothing due to the man whom we have all such reason to love, and no reason in the world to think ill of? To the possibility of motives unanswerable in themselves, though unavoidably secret for a while? And, after all, what is it you suspect him of?"

"I can hardly tell myself. But suspicion of something unpleasant is the inevitable consequence of such an alteration as we just witnessed in him. There is great truth, however, in what you have now urged of the allowances which ought to be made for him, and it is my wish to be candid in my judgment of every body. Willoughby may undoubtedly have very sufficient reasons for his conduct, and I will hope that he has. But it would have been more like Willoughby to acknowledge them at once. Secrecy may be advisable; but still I cannot help wondering at its being practiced by him."

"Do not blame him, however, for departing from his character, where the deviation is necessary. But you really do admit the justice of what I have said in his defence? – I am happy – and he is acquitted."

"Not entirely. It may be proper to conceal their engagement (if they **are** engaged) from Mrs. Smith – and if that is the case, it must be highly expedient for Willoughby to be but little in Devonshire at present. But this is no excuse for their concealing it from us."

"Concealing it from us! my dear child, do you accuse Willoughby and Marianne of concealment? This is strange indeed, when your eyes have been reproaching them every day for incautiousness."

"I want no proof of their affection," said Elinor; "but of their engagement I do."

"I am perfectly satisfied of both."

"Yet not a syllable has been said to you on the subject, by either of them."

"I have not wanted syllables where actions have spoken so plainly. Has not his behaviour to Marianne and to all of us, for at least the last fortnight, declared that he loved and considered her as his future wife, and that he felt for us the attachment of the nearest relation? Have we not perfectly understood each other? Has not my consent been daily asked by his looks, his manner, his attentive and affectionate respect? My Elinor, is it possible to doubt their engagement? How could such a thought occur to you? How is it to be supposed that Willoughby, persuaded as he must be of your sister's love, should leave her, and leave her perhaps for months, without telling her of his affection; – that they should part without a mutual exchange of confidence?"

"I confess," replied Elinor, "that every circumstance except **one** is in favour of their engagement; but that **one** is the total silence of both on the subject, and with me it almost outweighs every other."

"How strange this is! You must think wretchedly indeed of Willoughby, if, after all that has openly passed between them, you can doubt the nature of the terms on which they are together. Has he been acting a part in his behaviour to your sister all this time? Do you suppose him really indifferent to her?"

"No, I cannot think that. He must and does

love her I am sure."

"But with a strange kind of tenderness, if he can leave her with such indifference, such carelessness of the future, as you attribute to him."

"You must remember, my dear mother, that I have never considered this matter as certain. I have had my doubts, I confess; but they are fainter than they were, and they may soon be entirely done away. If we find they correspond, every fear of mine will be removed."

"A mighty concession indeed! If you were to see them at the altar, you would suppose they were going to be married. Ungracious girl! But I require no such proof. Nothing in my opinion has ever passed to justify doubt; no secrecy has been attempted; all has been uniformly open and unreserved. You cannot doubt your sister's wishes. It must be Willoughby therefore whom you suspect. But why? Is he not a man of honour and feeling? Has there been any inconsistency on his side to create alarm? can he be deceitful?"

"I hope not, I believe not," cried Elinor. "I love Willoughby, sincerely love him; and suspicion of his integrity cannot be more painful to yourself than to me. It has been involuntary, and I will not encourage it. I was startled, I confess, by the alteration in his manners this morning; – he did not speak like himself, and did not return your kindness with any cordiality. But all this may be explained by such a situation of his affairs as you have supposed. He had just parted from my sister, had seen her leave him in the greatest affliction; and if he felt obliged, from a fear of offending Mrs. Smith, to resist the temptation of returning here soon, and yet aware that by declining your invitation, by saying that he was going away for some time, he should seem to act an ungenerous, a suspicious part by our family, he might well be embarrassed and disturbed. In such a case, a plain and open avowal of his difficulties would have been more to his honour I think, as well as more consistent with his general character; – but I will not raise objections against any one's conduct on so illiberal a foundation, as a difference in judgment from myself, or a deviation from what I may think right and consistent."

"You speak very properly. Willoughby certainly does not deserve to be suspected. Though **we** have not known him long, he is no stranger in this part of the world; and who has ever spoken to his disadvantage? Had he been in a situation to act independently and marry immediately, it might have been odd that he should leave us without acknowledging everything to me at once: but this is not the case. It is an engagement in some respects not prosperously begun, for their marriage must be at a very uncertain distance; and even secrecy, as far as it can be observed, may now be very advisable."

They were interrupted by the entrance of

Margaret; and Elinor was then at liberty to think over the representations of her mother, to acknowledge the probability of many, and hope for the justice of all.

They saw nothing of Marianne till dinner time, when she entered the room and took her place at the table without saying a word. Her eyes were red and swollen; and it seemed as if her tears were even then restrained with difficulty. She avoided the looks of them all, could neither eat nor speak, and after some time, on her mother's silently pressing her hand with tender compassion, her small degree of fortitude was quite overcome, she burst into tears and left the room.

This violent oppression of spirits continued the whole evening. She was without any power, because she was without any desire of command over herself. The slightest mention of anything relative to Willoughby overpowered her in an instant; and though her family were most anxiously attentive to her comfort, it was impossible for them, if they spoke at all, to keep clear of every subject which her feelings connected with him.

CHAPTER SIXTEEN

MARIANNE WOULD HAVE THOUGHT herself very inexcusable had she been able to sleep at all the first night after parting from Willoughby. She would have been ashamed to look her family in the face the next morning, had she not risen from her bed in more need of repose than when she lay down in it. But the feelings which made such composure a disgrace, left her in no danger of incurring it. She was awake the whole night, and she wept the greatest part of it. She got up with a headache, was unable to talk, and unwilling to take any nourishment; giving pain every moment to her mother and sisters, and forbidding all attempt at consolation from either. Her sensibility was potent enough!

When breakfast was over she walked out by herself, and wandered about the village of Allenham, indulging the recollection of past enjoyment and crying over the present reverse for the chief of the morning.

The evening passed off in the equal indulgence of feeling. She played over every favourite song that she had been used to play to Willoughby, every air in which their voices had been oftenest joined, and sat at the instrument gazing on every line of music that he had written out for her, till her heart was so heavy that no farther sadness could be gained; and this nourishment of grief was every day applied. She spent whole hours at the pianoforte alternately singing and crying;

her voice often totally suspended by her tears. In books too, as well as in music, she courted the misery which a contrast between the past and present was certain of giving. She read nothing but what they had been used to read together.

Such violence of affliction indeed could not be supported for ever; it sunk within a few days into a calmer melancholy; but these employments, to which she daily recurred, her solitary walks and silent meditations, still produced occasional effusions of sorrow as lively as ever.

No letter from Willoughby came; and none seemed expected by Marianne. Her mother was surprised, and Elinor again became uneasy. But Mrs. Dashwood could find explanations whenever she wanted them, which at least satisfied herself.

"Remember, Elinor," said she, "how very often Sir John fetches our letters himself from the post, and carries them to it. We have already agreed that secrecy may be necessary, and we must acknowledge that it could not be maintained if their correspondence were to pass through Sir John's hands."

Elinor could not deny the truth of this, and she tried to find in it a motive sufficient for their silence. But there was one method so direct, so simple, and in her opinion so eligible of knowing the real state of the affair, and of instantly removing all mystery, that she could not help suggesting it to her mother.

"Why do you not ask Marianne at once," said she, "whether she is or she is not engaged to Willoughby? From you, her mother, and so kind, so indulgent a mother, the question could not give offence. It would be the natural result of your affection for her. She used to be all unreserve, and to you more especially."

"I would not ask such a question for the world. Supposing it possible that they are not engaged, what distress would not such an enquiry inflict! At any rate it would be most ungenerous. I should never deserve her confidence again, after forcing from her a confession of what is meant at present to be unacknowledged to any one. I know Marianne's heart: I know that she dearly loves me, and that I shall not be the last to whom the affair is made known, when circumstances make the revealment of it eligible. I would not attempt to force the confidence of any one; of a child much less; because a sense of duty would prevent the denial which her wishes might direct."

Elinor thought this generosity overstrained, considering her sister's youth, and urged the matter farther, but in vain; common sense, common care, common prudence, were all sunk in Mrs. Dashwood's romantic delicacy.

It was several days before Willoughby's name was mentioned before Marianne by any of her family; Sir John and Mrs. Jennings, indeed, were not so nice; their witticisms added pain to many a painful hour; – but one evening, Mrs. Dashwood, accidentally taking up a volume of Shakespeare, exclaimed,

"We have never finished Hamlet, Marianne; our dear Willoughby went away before we could get through it. We will put it by, that when he comes again...But it may be months, perhaps, before **that** happens."

"Months!" cried Marianne, with strong surprise. "No – nor many weeks."

Mrs. Dashwood was sorry for what she had said; but it gave Elinor pleasure, as it produced a reply from Marianne so expressive of confidence in Willoughby and knowledge of his intentions.

One morning, about a week after his leaving the country, Marianne was prevailed on to join her sisters in their usual walk, instead of wandering away by herself. Hitherto she had carefully avoided every companion in her rambles. If her sisters intended to walk on the downs, she directly stole away towards the lanes; if they talked of the valley, she was as speedy in climbing the hills, and could never be found when the others set off. But at length she was secured by the exertions of Elinor, who greatly disapproved such continual seclusion. They walked along the road through the valley, and chiefly in silence, for Marianne's **mind** could not be controlled, and Elinor, satisfied with gaining one point, would not then attempt more. Beyond the entrance of the valley, where the country, though still rich, was less wild and more open, a long stretch of the road which they had travelled on first coming to Barton, lay before them; and on reaching that point, they stopped to look around them, and examine a prospect which formed the distance of their view from the cottage, from a spot which they had never happened to reach in any of their walks before.

Amongst the objects in the scene, they soon discovered an animated one; it was a man on horseback riding towards them. In a few minutes they could distinguish him to be a gentleman; and in a moment afterwards Marianne rapturously exclaimed,

"It is he; it is indeed; – I know it is!" – and was hastening to meet him, when Elinor cried out,

"Indeed, Marianne, I think you are mistaken. It is not Willoughby. The person is not tall enough for him, and has not his air."

"He has, he has," cried Marianne, "I am sure he has. His air, his coat, his horse. I knew how soon he would come."

She walked eagerly on as she spoke; and Elinor, to screen Marianne from particularity, as she felt almost certain of its not being Willoughby, quickened her pace and kept up with her. They were soon within thirty yards of the gentleman. Marianne looked again; her heart sunk within her; and abruptly turning round, she was hurrying back, when the voices of both her sisters were raised to detain her; a third, almost as well known as Willoughby's, joined them in begging her to stop, and she turned round with surprise to see and welcome Edward Ferrars.

He was the only person in the world who could at that moment be forgiven for not being Willoughby; the only one who could have gained a smile from her; but she dispersed her tears to smile on **him**, and in her sister's happiness forgot for a time her own disappointment.

He dismounted, and giving his horse to his servant, walked back with them to Barton, whither he was purposely coming to visit them.

He was welcomed by them all with great cordiality, but especially by Marianne, who showed more warmth of regard in her reception of him than even Elinor herself. To Marianne, indeed, the meeting between Edward and her sister was but a continuation of that unaccountable coldness which she had often observed at Norland in their mutual behaviour. On Edward's side, more particularly, there was a deficiency of all that a lover ought to look and say on such an occasion. He was confused, seemed scarcely sensible of pleasure in seeing them, looked neither rapturous nor gay, said little but what was forced from him by questions, and distinguished Elinor by no mark of affection. Marianne saw and listened with increasing surprise. She began almost to feel a dislike of Edward; and it ended, as every feeling must end with her, by carrying back her thoughts to Willoughby, whose manners formed a contrast sufficiently striking to those of his brother elect.

After a short silence which succeeded the first surprise and enquiries of meeting, Marianne asked Edward if he came directly from London. No, he had been in Devonshire a fortnight.

"A fortnight!" she repeated, surprised at his being so long in the same county with Elinor without seeing her before.

He looked rather distressed as he added, that he had been staying with some friends near Plymouth.

"Have you been lately in Sussex?" said Elinor.

"I was at Norland about a month ago."

"And how does dear, dear Norland look?" cried Marianne.

"Dear, dear Norland," said Elinor, "probably looks much as it always does at this time of the year. The woods and walks thickly covered with dead leaves."

"Oh," cried Marianne, "with what transporting sensation have I formerly seen them fall! How have I delighted, as I walked, to see them driven in showers about me by the wind! What feelings have they, the season, the air altogether inspired! Now there is no one to regard them. They are seen only as a nuisance, swept hastily off, and driven as much as possible from the sight."

"It is not every one," said Elinor, "who has

your passion for dead leaves."

"No; my feelings are not often shared, not often understood. But **sometimes** they are." – As she said this, she sunk into a reverie for a few moments; – but rousing herself again, "Now, Edward," said she, calling his attention to the prospect, "here is Barton valley. Look up to it, and be tranquil if you can. Look at those hills! Did you ever see their equals? To the left is Barton park, amongst those woods and plantations. You may see the end of the house. And there, beneath that farthest hill, which rises with such grandeur, is our cottage."

"It is a beautiful country," he replied; "but these bottoms must be dirty in winter."

"How can you think of dirt, with such objects before you?"

"Because," replied he, smiling, "among the rest of the objects before me, I see a very dirty lane."

"How strange!" said Marianne to herself as she walked on.

"Have you an agreeable neighbourhood here? Are the Middletons pleasant people?"

"No, not all," answered Marianne; "we could not be more unfortunately situated."

"Marianne," cried her sister, "how can you say so? How can you be so unjust? They are a very respectable family, Mr. Ferrars; and towards us have behaved in the friendliest manner. Have you forgot, Marianne, how many pleasant days we have owed to them?"

"No," said Marianne, in a low voice, "nor how many painful moments."

Elinor took no notice of this; and directing her attention to their visitor, endeavoured to support something like discourse with him, by talking of their present residence, its conveniences, &c. extorting from him occasional questions and remarks. His coldness and reserve mortified her severely; she was vexed and half angry; but resolving to regulate her behaviour to him by the past rather than the present, she avoided every appearance of resentment or displeasure, and treated him as she thought he ought to be treated from the family connection.

CHAPTER SEVENTEEN

MRS. DASHWOOD was surprised only for a moment at seeing him; for his coming to Barton was, in her opinion, of all things the most natural. Her joy and expression of regard long outlived her wonder. He received the kindest welcome from her; and shyness, coldness, reserve could not stand against such a reception. They had begun to fail him before he entered the house, and they were quite overcome by the captivating manners of Mrs. Dashwood.

Indeed a man could not very well be in love with either of her daughters, without extending the passion to her; and Elinor had the satisfaction of seeing him soon become more like himself. His affections seemed to reanimate towards them all, and his interest in their welfare again became perceptible. He was not in spirits, however; he praised their house, admired its prospect, was attentive, and kind; but still he was not in spirits. The whole family perceived it, and Mrs. Dashwood, attributing it to some want of liberality in his mother, sat down to table indignant against all selfish parents.

"What are Mrs. Ferrars's views for you at present, Edward?" said she, when dinner was over and they had drawn round the fire; "are you still to be a great orator in spite of yourself?"

"No. I hope my mother is now convinced that I have no more talents than inclination for a public life!"

"But how is your fame to be established? for famous you must be to satisfy all your family; and with no inclination for expense, no affection for strangers, no profession, and no assurance, you may find it a difficult matter."

"I shall not attempt it. I have no wish to be distinguished; and have every reason to hope I never shall. Thank Heaven! I cannot be forced into genius and eloquence."

"You have no ambition, I well know. Your wishes are all moderate."

"As moderate as those of the rest of the world, I believe. I wish as well as every body else to be perfectly happy; but, like every body else it must be in my own way. Greatness will not make me so."

"Strange that it would!" cried Marianne. "What have wealth or grandeur to do with happiness?"

"Grandeur has but little," said Elinor, "but wealth has much to do with it."

"Elinor, for shame!" said Marianne, "money

can only give happiness where there is nothing else to give it. Beyond a competence, it can afford no real satisfaction, as far as mere self is concerned."

"Perhaps," said Elinor, smiling, "we may come to the same point. **your** competence and **my** wealth are very much alike, I dare say; and without them, as the world goes now, we shall both agree that every kind of external comfort must be wanting. Your ideas are only more noble than mine. Come, what is your competence?"

"About eighteen hundred or two thousand a year; not more than **that**."

Elinor laughed. "**Two** thousand a year! **One** is my wealth! I guessed how it would end."

"And yet two thousand a-year is a very moderate income," said Marianne. "A family cannot well be maintained on a smaller. I am sure I am not extravagant in my demands. A proper establishment of servants, a carriage, perhaps two, and hunters, cannot be supported on less."

Elinor smiled again, to hear her sister describing so accurately their future expenses at Combe Magna.

"Hunters!" repeated Edward – "but why must you have hunters? Every body does not hunt."

Marianne coloured as she replied, "But most people do."

"I wish," said Margaret, striking out a novel thought, "that somebody would give us all a large fortune apiece!"

"Oh that they would!" cried Marianne, her eyes sparkling with animation, and her cheeks glowing with the delight of such imaginary happiness.

"We are all unanimous in that wish, I suppose," said Elinor, "in spite of the insufficiency of wealth."

"Oh dear!" cried Margaret, "how happy I should be! I wonder what I should do with it!"

Marianne looked as if she had no doubt

on that point.

"I should be puzzled to spend so large a fortune myself," said Mrs. Dashwood, "if my children were all to be rich without my help."

"You must begin your improvements on this house," observed Elinor, "and your difficulties will soon vanish."

"What magnificent orders would travel from this family to London," said Edward, "in such an event! What a happy day for booksellers, music-sellers, and print-shops! You, Miss Dashwood, would give a general commission for every new print of merit to be sent you – and as for Marianne, I know her greatness of soul, there would not be music enough in London to content her. And books! – Thomson, Cowper, Scott – she would buy them all over and over again: she would buy up every copy, I believe, to prevent their falling into unworthy hands; and she would have every book that tells her how to admire an old twisted tree. Should not you, Marianne? Forgive me, if I am very saucy. But I was willing to shew you that I had not forgot our old disputes."

"I love to be reminded of the past, Edward – whether it be melancholy or gay, I love to recall it – and you will never offend me by talking of former times. You are very right in supposing how my money would be spent – some of it, at least – my loose cash would certainly be employed in improving my collection of music and books."

"And the bulk of your fortune would be laid out in annuities on the authors or their heirs."

"No, Edward, I should have something else to do with it."

"Perhaps, then, you would bestow it as a reward on that person who wrote the ablest defence of your favourite maxim, that no one can ever be in love more than once in their life – your opinion on that point is unchanged, I presume?"

"Undoubtedly. At my time of life opinions are tolerably fixed. It is not likely that I should now see or hear any thing to change them."

"Marianne is as steadfast as ever, you see," said Elinor, "she is not at all altered."

"She is only grown a little more grave than she was."

"Nay, Edward," said Marianne, "you need not reproach me. You are not very gay yourself."

"Why should you think so!" replied he, with a sigh. "But gaiety never was a part of **my** character."

"Nor do I think it a part of Marianne's," said Elinor; "I should hardly call her a lively girl – she is very earnest, very eager in all she does – sometimes talks a great deal and always with animation – but she is not often really merry."

"I believe you are right," he replied, "and yet I have always set her down as a lively girl."

"I have frequently detected myself in such kind of mistakes," said Elinor, "in a total misapprehension of character in some point or other: fancying people so much more gay or grave, or ingenious or stupid than they really are, and I can hardly tell why or in what the deception originated. Sometimes one is guided by what they say of themselves, and very frequently by what other people say of them, without giving oneself time to deliberate and judge."

"But I thought it was right, Elinor," said Marianne, "to be guided wholly by the opinion of other people. I thought our judgments were given us merely to be subservient to those of neighbours. This has always been your doctrine, I am sure."

"No, Marianne, never. My doctrine has never aimed at the subjection of the understanding. All I have ever attempted to influence has been the behaviour. You must not confound my meaning. I am guilty, I confess, of having often wished you to treat our acquaintance in general with greater attention; but when have I advised you to adopt their sentiments or to conform to their judgment in serious matters?"

"You have not been able to bring your sister over to your plan of general civility," said Edward to Elinor, "Do you gain no ground?"

"Quite the contrary," replied Elinor, looking expressively at Marianne.

"My judgment," he returned, "is all on your side of the question; but I am afraid my practice is much more on your sister's. I never wish to offend, but I am so foolishly shy, that I often seem negligent, when I am only kept back by my natural awkwardness. I have frequently thought that I must have been intended by nature to be fond of low company, I am so little at my ease among strangers of gentility!"

"Marianne has not shyness to excuse any inattention of hers," said Elinor.

"She knows her own worth too well for false shame," replied Edward. "Shyness is only the effect of a sense of inferiority in some way or other. If I could persuade myself that my manners were perfectly easy and graceful, I should not be shy."

"But you would still be reserved," said Marianne, "and that is worse."

Edward started – "Reserved! Am I reserved, Marianne?"

"Yes, very."

"I do not understand you," replied he, colouring. "Reserved! – how, in what manner? What am I to tell you? What can you suppose?"

Elinor looked surprised at his emotion; but trying to laugh off the subject, she said to him, "Do not you know my sister well enough to understand what she means? Do not you know she calls every one reserved who does not talk as fast, and admire what she admires as rapturously as herself?"

Edward made no answer. His gravity and thoughtfulness returned on him in their fullest extent – and he sat for some time silent and dull.

CHAPTER EIGHTEEN

ELINOR SAW, with great uneasiness the low spirits of her friend. His visit afforded her but a very partial satisfaction, while his own enjoyment in it appeared so imperfect. It was evident that he was unhappy; she wished it were equally evident that he still distinguished her by the same affection which once she had felt no doubt of inspiring; but hitherto the continuance of his preference seemed very uncertain; and the reservedness of his manner towards her contradicted one moment what a more animated look had intimated the preceding one.

He joined her and Marianne in the breakfast-room the next morning before the others were down; and Marianne, who was always eager to promote their happiness as far as she could, soon left them to themselves. But before she was half way upstairs she heard the parlour door open, and, turning round, was astonished to see Edward himself come out.

“I am going into the village to see my horses,” said he, “as you are not yet ready for breakfast; I shall be back again presently.”

Edward returned to them with fresh admiration of the surrounding country; in his walk to the village, he had seen many parts of the valley to advantage; and the village itself, in a much higher situation than the cottage, afforded a general view of the whole, which had exceedingly pleased him. This was a subject which ensured Marianne's attention, and she was beginning to describe her own admiration of these scenes, and to question him more minutely on the objects that had particularly struck him, when Edward interrupted her by saying, "You must not enquire too far, Marianne – remember I have no knowledge in the picturesque, and I shall offend you by my ignorance and want of taste if we come to particulars. I shall call hills steep, which ought to be bold; surfaces strange and uncouth, which ought to be irregular and rugged; and distant objects out of sight, which ought only to be indistinct through the soft medium of a hazy atmosphere. You must be satisfied with such admiration as I can honestly give. I call it a very fine country – the hills are steep, the woods seem full of fine timber, and the valley looks comfortable and snug – with rich meadows and several neat farm houses scattered here and there. It exactly answers my idea of a fine country, because it unites beauty with utility – and I dare say it is a picturesque one too, because you admire it; I can easily believe it to be full of rocks and promontories, grey moss and brush wood, but these are all lost on me. I know nothing of the picturesque."

"I am afraid it is but too true," said Marianne; "but why should you boast of it?"

"I suspect," said Elinor, "that to avoid one kind of affectation, Edward here falls into another. Because he believes many people pretend to more admiration of the beauties of nature than they really feel, and is disgusted with such pretensions, he affects greater indifference and less discrimination in viewing them himself than he possesses. He is fastidious and will have an affectation of his own."

"It is very true," said Marianne, "that admiration of landscape scenery is become a mere jargon. Every body pretends to feel and tries to describe with the taste and elegance of him who first defined what picturesque beauty was. I detest jargon of every kind, and sometimes I have kept my feelings to myself, because I could find no language to describe them in but what was worn and hackneyed out of all sense and meaning."

"I am convinced," said Edward, "that you really feel all the delight in a fine prospect which you profess to feel. But, in return, your sister must allow me to feel no more than I profess. I like a fine prospect, but not on picturesque principles. I do not like crooked, twisted, blasted trees. I admire them much more if they are tall, straight, and flourishing. I do not like ruined, tattered cottages. I am not fond of nettles or thistles, or heath blossoms. I have more pleasure in a snug farm-house than a watch-tower – and a troop of tidy, happy villages please me better than the finest banditti in the world."

Marianne looked with amazement at Edward, with compassion at her sister. Elinor only laughed.

Chapter Eighteen

The subject was continued no farther; and Marianne remained thoughtfully silent, till a new object suddenly engaged her attention. She was sitting by Edward, and in taking his tea from Mrs. Dashwood, his hand passed so directly before her, as to make a ring, with a plait of hair in the centre, very conspicuous on one of his fingers.

"I never saw you wear a ring before, Edward," she cried. "Is that Fanny's hair? I remember her promising to give you some. But I should have thought her hair had been darker."

Marianne spoke inconsiderately what she really felt – but when she saw how much she had pained Edward, her own vexation at her want of thought could not be surpassed by his. He coloured very deeply, and giving a momentary glance at Elinor, replied, "Yes; it is my sister's hair. The setting always casts a different shade on it, you know."

Elinor had met his eye, and looked conscious likewise. That the hair was her own, she instantaneously felt as well satisfied as Marianne; the only difference in their conclusions was, that what Marianne considered as a free gift from her sister, Elinor was conscious must have been procured by some theft or contrivance unknown to herself. She was not in a humour, however, to regard it as an affront, and affecting to take no notice of what passed, by instantly talking of something else, she internally resolved henceforward to catch every opportunity of eyeing the hair and of satisfying herself, beyond all doubt, that it was exactly the shade of her own.

Edward's embarrassment lasted some time, and it ended in an absence of mind still more settled. He was particularly grave the whole morning. Marianne severely censured herself for what she had said; but her own forgiveness might have been more speedy, had she known how little offence it had given her sister.

Before the middle of the day, they were visited by Sir John and Mrs. Jennings, who, having heard of the arrival of a gentleman at the cottage, came to take a survey of the guest. With the assistance of his mother-in-law, Sir John was not long in discovering that the name of Ferrars began with an F. and this prepared a future mine of raillery against the devoted Elinor, which nothing but the newness of their acquaintance with Edward could have prevented from being immediately sprung. But, as it was, she only learned, from some very significant looks, how far their penetration, founded on Margaret's instructions, extended.

Sir John never came to the Dashwoods without either inviting them to dine at the park the next day, or to drink tea with them that evening. On the present occasion, for the better entertainment of their visitor, towards whose amusement he felt himself bound to contribute, he wished to engage them for both.

"You **must** drink tea with us to night," said he, "for we shall be quite alone – and tomorrow you must absolutely dine with us, for we shall be a large party."

Mrs. Jennings enforced the necessity. "And who knows but you may raise a dance," said she. "And that will tempt **you**, Miss Marianne."

"A dance!" cried Marianne. "Impossible! Who is to dance?"

"Who! why yourselves, and the Careys, and Whitakers to be sure. – What! you thought nobody could dance because a certain person that shall be nameless is gone!"

"I wish with all my soul," cried Sir John, "that Willoughby were among us again."

This, and Marianne's blushing, gave new suspicions to Edward. "And who is Willoughby?" said he, in a low voice, to Miss Dashwood, by whom he was sitting.

She gave him a brief reply. Marianne's countenance was more communicative. Edward saw enough to comprehend, not only the meaning of others, but such of

Marianne's expressions as had puzzled him before; and when their visitors left them, he went immediately round her, and said, in a whisper, "I have been guessing. Shall I tell you my guess?"

"What do you mean?"

"Shall I tell you."

"Certainly."

"Well then; I guess that Mr. Willoughby hunts."

Marianne was surprised and confused, yet she could not help smiling at the quiet archness of his manner, and after a moment's silence, said, "Oh, Edward! How can you? – But the time will come I hope...I am sure you will like him."

"I do not doubt it," replied he, rather astonished at her earnestness and warmth; for had he not imagined it to be a joke for the good of her acquaintance in general, founded only on a something or a nothing between Mr. Willoughby and herself, he would not have ventured to mention it.

CHAPTER NINETEEN

EDWARD REMAINED a week at the cottage; he was earnestly pressed by Mrs. Dashwood to stay longer; but, as if he were bent only on self-mortification, he seemed resolved to be gone when his enjoyment among his friends was at the height. His spirits, during the last two or three days, though still very unequal, were greatly improved – he grew more and more partial to the house and environs – never spoke of going away without a sigh – declared his time to be wholly disengaged – even doubted to what place he should go when he left them – but still, go he must. Never had any week passed so quickly – he could hardly believe it to be gone. He said so repeatedly; other things he said too, which marked the turn of his feelings and gave the lie to his actions. He had no pleasure at Norland; he detested being in town; but either to Norland or London, he must go. He valued their kindness beyond any thing, and his greatest happiness was in being with them. Yet, he must leave them at the end of a week, in spite of their wishes and his own, and without any restraint on his time.

Elinor placed all that was astonishing in this way of acting to his mother's account; and it was happy for her that he had a mother whose character was so imperfectly known to her, as to be the general excuse for every thing strange on the part of her son. Disappointed, however, and vexed as she was, and sometimes displeased with his uncertain behaviour to herself, she was very well disposed on the whole to regard his actions with all the candid allowances and generous qualifications, which had been rather more painfully extorted from her, for Willoughby's service, by her mother. His want of spirits, of openness, and of consistency, were most usually attributed to his want of independence, and his better knowledge of Mrs. Ferrars's disposition and designs. The shortness of his visit, the steadiness of his purpose in leaving them, originated in the same fettered inclination, the same inevitable necessity of temporizing with his mother. The old well-established grievance of duty against will, parent against child, was the cause of all. She would have been glad to know when these difficulties were to cease, this opposition was to yield, – when Mrs. Ferrars would be reformed, and her son be at liberty to be happy. But from such vain wishes she was forced to turn for comfort to the renewal of her confidence in Edward's affection, to the remembrance of every mark of regard in look or word which fell from him while at Barton, and above all to that flattering proof of it which he constantly wore round his finger.

"I think, Edward," said Mrs. Dashwood, as they were at breakfast the last morning, "you would be a happier man if you had any profession to engage your time and give an interest to your plans and actions. Some inconvenience to your friends, indeed, might result from it – you would not be able to give them so much of your time. But (with a smile) you would be materially benefited in one particular at least – you would know where to go when you left them."

"I do assure you," he replied, "that I have long thought on this point, as you think now. It has been, and is, and probably will always be a heavy misfortune to me, that I have had no necessary business to engage me, no profession to give me employment, or afford me any thing like independence. But unfortunately my own nicety, and the nicety of my friends, have made me what I am, an idle, helpless being. We never could agree in our choice of a profession. I always preferred the church, as I still do. But that was not smart enough for my family. They recommended the army. That was a great deal too smart for me. The law was allowed to be genteel enough; many young men, who had chambers in the Temple, made a very good appearance in the first circles, and drove about town in very knowing gigs. But I had no inclination for the law, even in this less abstruse study of it, which my family approved. As for the navy, it had fashion on its side, but I was too old when the subject was first started to enter it – and, at length, as there was no necessity for my having any profession at all, as I might be as dashing and expensive without a red coat on my back as with one, idleness was pronounced on the whole to be most advantageous and honourable, and a young man of eighteen is not in general so earnestly bent on being busy as to resist the solicitations of his friends to do nothing. I was therefore entered at Oxford and have been properly idle ever since."

"The consequence of which, I suppose, will be," said Mrs. Dashwood, "since leisure has not promoted your own happiness, that your sons will be brought up to as many pursuits, employments, professions, and trades as Columella's."

"They will be brought up," said he, in a serious accent, "to be as unlike myself as is possible. In feeling, in action, in condition, in every thing."

"Come, come; this is all an effusion of immediate want of spirits, Edward. You are in a melancholy humour, and fancy that any one unlike yourself must be happy. But remember that the pain of parting from friends will be felt by every body at times, whatever be their education or state. Know your own happiness. You want nothing but patience – or give it a more fascinating name, call it hope. Your mother will secure to you, in time, that independence you are so anxious for; it is her duty, and it will, it must ere long become her happiness to prevent your whole youth from being wasted in discontent. How much may not a few months do?"

"I think," replied Edward, "that I may defy many months to produce any good to me."

This desponding turn of mind, though it could not be communicated to Mrs. Dashwood, gave additional pain to them all in the parting, which shortly took place, and left an uncomfortable impression on Elinor's feelings especially, which required some trouble and time to subdue. But as it was her determination to subdue it, and to prevent herself from appearing to suffer more than what all her family suffered on his going away, she did not adopt the method so judiciously employed by Marianne, on a similar occasion, to augment and fix her sorrow, by seeking silence, solitude and idleness. Their means were as different as their objects, and equally suited to the advancement of each.

Elinor sat down to her drawing-table as soon as he was out of the house, busily employed herself the whole day, neither sought nor avoided the mention of his name, appeared to interest herself almost as much as ever in the general concerns of the family, and if, by this conduct, she did not lessen her own grief, it was at least prevented from unnecessary increase, and her mother and sisters were spared much solicitude on her account.

Such behaviour as this, so exactly the reverse of her own, appeared no more meritorious to Marianne, than her own had seemed faulty to her. The business of self-command she settled very easily; – with strong affections it was impossible, with calm ones it could have no merit. That her sister's affections **were** calm, she dared not deny, though she blushed to acknowledge it; and of the strength of her own, she gave a very striking proof, by still loving and respecting that sister, in spite of this mortifying conviction.

Without shutting herself up from her family, or leaving the house in determined solitude to avoid them, or lying awake the whole night to indulge meditation, Elinor found every day afforded her leisure enough to think of Edward, and of Edward's behaviour, in every possible variety which the different state of her spirits at different times could produce, – with tenderness, pity, approbation, censure, and doubt. There were moments in abundance, when, if not by the absence of her mother and sisters, at least by the nature of their employments, conversation was forbidden among them, and every effect of solitude was produced. Her mind was inevitably at liberty; her thoughts could not be chained elsewhere; and the past and the future, on a subject so interesting, must be before her, must force her attention, and engross her memory, her reflection, and her fancy.

From a reverie of this kind, as she sat at her drawing-table, she was roused one morning, soon after Edward's leaving them, by the arrival of company. She happened to be quite alone. The closing of the little gate, at the entrance of the green court in front of the house, drew her eyes to the window, and she saw a large party walking up to the door. Amongst them were Sir John and Lady Middleton and Mrs. Jennings, but there were two others, a gentleman and lady, who were quite unknown to her. She was sitting near the window, and as soon as Sir John perceived her, he left the rest of the party to the ceremony of knocking at the door, and stepping across the turf, obliged her to open the casement to speak to him, though the space was so short between the door and the window, as to make it hardly possible to speak at one without being heard at the other.

"Well," said he, "we have brought you some strangers. How do you like them?"

"Hush! they will hear you."

"Never mind if they do. It is only the Palmers. Charlotte is very pretty, I can tell you. You may see her if you look this way."

As Elinor was certain of seeing her in a couple of minutes, without taking that liberty, she begged to be excused.

"Where is Marianne? Has she run away because we are come? I see her instrument is open."

"She is walking, I believe."

They were now joined by Mrs. Jennings, who had not patience enough to wait till the door was opened before she told **her** story. She came hallooing to the window, "How do you do, my dear? How does Mrs. Dashwood do? And where are your sisters? What! all alone! you will be glad of a little company to sit with you. I have brought my other son and daughter to see you. Only think of their coming so suddenly! I thought I heard a carriage last night, while we were drinking our tea, but it never entered my head that it could be them. I thought of nothing but whether it might not be Colonel Brandon come back again; so I said to Sir John, I do think I hear a carriage; perhaps it is Colonel Brandon come back again" –

Elinor was obliged to turn from her, in the middle of her story, to receive the rest of the party; Lady Middleton introduced the two strangers; Mrs. Dashwood and Margaret came down stairs at the same time, and they all sat down to look at one another, while Mrs. Jennings continued her story as she walked through the passage into the parlour, attended by Sir John.

Mrs. Palmer was several years younger than Lady Middleton, and totally unlike her in every respect. She was short and plump, had a very pretty face, and the finest expression of good humour in it that could possibly be. Her manners were by no means so elegant as her sister's, but they were much more prepossessing. She came in with a smile, smiled all the time of her visit, except when she laughed, and smiled when she went away. Her husband was a grave looking young man of five or six and twenty, with an air of more fashion and sense than his wife, but of less willingness to please or be pleased. He entered the room with a look of self-consequence, slightly bowed to the ladies, without speaking a word, and, after briefly surveying them and their apartments, took up a newspaper from the table, and continued to read it as long as he staid.

Mrs. Palmer, on the contrary, who was strongly endowed by nature with a turn for being uniformly civil and happy, was hardly seated before her admiration of the parlour and every thing in it burst forth.

"Well! what a delightful room this is! I never saw anything so charming! Only think, Mama, how it is improved since I was here last! I always thought it such a sweet place, ma'am! (turning to Mrs. Dashwood) but you have made it so charming! Only look, sister, how delightful every thing is! How I should like such a house for myself! Should not you, Mr. Palmer?"

Mr. Palmer made her no answer, and did not even raise his eyes from the newspaper.

"Mr. Palmer does not hear me," said she, laughing; "he never does sometimes. It is so ridiculous!"

This was quite a new idea to Mrs. Dashwood; she had never been used to find wit in the inattention of any one, and could not help looking with surprise at them both.

Mrs. Jennings, in the meantime, talked on as loud as she could, and continued her account of their surprise, the evening before, on seeing their friends, without ceasing till every thing was told. Mrs. Palmer laughed heartily at the recollection of their astonishment, and every body agreed, two or three times over, that it had been quite an agreeable surprise.

"You may believe how glad we all were to see them," added Mrs. Jennings, leaning forward towards Elinor, and speaking in a low voice as if she meant to be heard by no one else, though they were seated on different sides of the room; "but, however, I can't help wishing they had not travelled quite so fast, nor made such a long journey of it, for they came all round by London upon account of some business, for you know (nodding significantly and pointing to her daughter) it was wrong in her situation. I wanted her to stay at home and rest this morning, but she would come with us; she longed so much to see you all!"

Mrs. Palmer laughed, and said it would not do her any harm.

"She expects to be confined in February," continued Mrs. Jennings.

Lady Middleton could no longer endure such a conversation, and therefore exerted herself to ask Mr. Palmer if there was any news in the paper.

"No, none at all," he replied, and read on.

"Here comes Marianne," cried Sir John. "Now, Palmer, you shall see a monstrous pretty girl."

He immediately went into the passage, opened the front door, and ushered her in himself. Mrs. Jennings asked her, as soon as she appeared, if she had not been to Allenham; and Mrs. Palmer laughed so heartily at the question, as to show she understood it. Mr. Palmer looked up on her entering the room, stared at her some minutes, and then returned to his newspaper. Mrs. Palmer's eye was now caught by the drawings which hung round the room. She got up to examine them.

"Oh! dear, how beautiful these are! Well! how delightful! Do but look, mama, how sweet! I declare they are quite charming; I could look at them for ever." And then sitting down again, she very soon forgot that there were any such things in the room.

When Lady Middleton rose to go away, Mr. Palmer rose also, laid down the newspaper, stretched himself and looked at them all around.

"My love, have you been asleep?" said his wife, laughing.

He made her no answer; and only observed, after again examining the room, that it was very low pitched, and that the ceiling was crooked. He then made his bow, and departed with the rest.

Sir John had been very urgent with them all to spend the next day at the park. Mrs. Dashwood, who did not chuse to dine with them oftener than they dined at the cottage, absolutely refused on her own account; her daughters might do as they pleased. But they had no curiosity to see how Mr. and Mrs. Palmer ate their dinner, and no expectation of pleasure from them in any other way. They attempted, therefore, likewise, to excuse themselves; the weather was uncertain, and not likely to be good. But Sir John would not be satisfied – the carriage should be sent for them and they must come. Lady Middleton too, though she did not press their mother, pressed them. Mrs. Jennings and Mrs. Palmer joined their entreaties, all seemed equally anxious to avoid a family party; and the young ladies were obliged to yield.

"Why should they ask us?" said Marianne, as soon as they were gone. "The rent of this cottage is said to be low; but we have it on very hard terms, if we are to dine at the park whenever any one is staying either with them, or with us."

"They mean no less to be civil and kind to us now," said Elinor, "by these frequent invitations, than by those which we received from them a few weeks ago. The alteration is not in them, if their parties are grown tedious and dull. We must look for the change elsewhere."

CHAPTER TWENTY

AS THE MISS DASHWOODS entered the drawing-room of the park the next day, at one door, Mrs. Palmer came running in at the other, looking as good humoured and merry as before. She took them all most affectionately by the hand, and expressed great delight in seeing them again.

"I am so glad to see you!" said she, seating herself between Elinor and Marianne, "for it is so bad a day I was afraid you might not come, which would be a shocking thing, as we go away again tomorrow. We must go, for the Westons come to us next week you know. It was quite a sudden thing our coming at all, and I knew nothing of it till the carriage was coming to the door, and then Mr. Palmer asked me if I would go with him to Barton. He is so droll! He never tells me any thing! I am so sorry we cannot stay longer; however we shall meet again in town very soon, I hope."

They were obliged to put an end to such an expectation.

"Not go to town!" cried Mrs. Palmer, with a laugh, "I shall be quite disappointed if you do not. I could get the nicest house in the world for you, next door to ours, in Hanover-square. You must come, indeed. I am sure I shall be very happy to chaperon you at any time till I am confined, if Mrs. Dashwood should not like to go into public."

They thanked her; but were obliged to resist all her entreaties.

"Oh, my love," cried Mrs. Palmer to her

husband, who just then entered the room – "you must help me to persuade the Miss Dashwoods to go to town this winter."

Her love made no answer; and after slightly bowing to the ladies, began complaining of the weather.

"How horrid all this is!" said he. "Such weather makes every thing and every body disgusting. Dullness is as much produced within doors as without, by rain. It makes one detest all one's acquaintance. What the devil does Sir John mean by not having a billiard room in his house? How few people know what comfort is! Sir John is as stupid as the weather."

The rest of the company soon dropt in.

"I am afraid, Miss Marianne," said Sir John, "you have not been able to take your usual walk to Allenham today."

Marianne looked very grave and said nothing.

"Oh, don't be so sly before us," said Mrs. Palmer; "for we know all about it, I assure you; and I admire your taste very much, for I think he is extremely handsome. We do not live a great way from him in the country, you know. Not above ten miles, I dare say."

"Much nearer thirty," said her husband.

"Ah, well! there is not much difference. I never was at his house; but they say it is a sweet pretty place."

"As vile a spot as I ever saw in my life," said Mr. Palmer.

Marianne remained perfectly silent, though her countenance betrayed her interest in what was said.

"Is it very ugly?" continued Mrs. Palmer – "then it must be some other place that is so pretty I suppose."

When they were seated in the dining room, Sir John observed with regret that they were only eight all together.

"My dear," said he to his lady, "it is very provoking that we should be so few. Why did not you ask the Gilberts to come to us today?"

"Did not I tell you, Sir John, when you spoke to me about it before, that it could not be done? They dined with us last."

"You and I, Sir John," said Mrs. Jennings, "should not stand upon such ceremony."

"Then you would be very ill-bred," cried Mr. Palmer.

"My love you contradict every body," said his wife with her usual laugh. "Do you know that you are quite rude?"

"I did not know I contradicted any body in calling your mother ill-bred."

"Ay, you may abuse me as you please," said the good-natured old lady, "you have taken Charlotte off my hands, and cannot give her back again. So there I have the whip hand of you."

Charlotte laughed heartily to think that her husband could not get rid of her; and exultingly said, she did not care how cross he was to her, as they must live together. It was impossible for any one to be more thoroughly good-natured, or more determined to be happy than Mrs. Palmer. The studied indifference, insolence, and discontent of her husband gave her no pain; and when he scolded or abused her, she was highly diverted.

"Mr. Palmer is so droll!" said she, in a whisper, to Elinor. "He is always out of humour."

Elinor was not inclined, after a little observation, to give him credit for being so genuinely and unaffectedly ill-natured or ill-bred as he wished to appear. His temper might perhaps be a little soured by finding, like many others of his sex, that through some unaccountable bias in favour of beauty, he was the husband of a very silly woman, – but she knew that this kind of blunder was too common for any sensible man to be lastingly hurt by it. – It was rather a wish of distinction, she believed, which produced his contemptuous treatment of every body, and his general abuse of every thing before him. It was the desire of appearing superior to other people. The motive was too common to be wondered at; but the means, however they might succeed by establishing his superiority in ill-breeding, were not likely to attach any one to him except his wife.

"Oh, my dear Miss Dashwood," said Mrs. Palmer soon afterwards, "I have got such a favour to ask of you and your sister. Will you come and spend some time at Cleveland this Christmas? Now, pray do, – and come while the Westons are with us. You cannot think how happy I shall be! It will be quite delightful! – My love," applying to her husband, "don't you long to have the Miss Dashwoods come to Cleveland?"

"Certainly," he replied, with a sneer – "I came into Devonshire with no other view."

"There now," – said his lady, "you see Mr. Palmer expects you; so you cannot refuse to come."

They both eagerly and resolutely declined her invitation.

"But indeed you must and shall come.

I am sure you will like it of all things. The Westons will be with us, and it will be quite delightful. You cannot think what a sweet place Cleveland is; and we are so gay now, for Mr. Palmer is always going about the country canvassing against the election; and so many people came to dine with us that I never saw before, it is quite charming! But, poor fellow! it is very fatiguing to him! for he is forced to make every body like him."

Elinor could hardly keep her countenance as she assented to the hardship of such an obligation.

"How charming it will be," said Charlotte, "when he is in Parliament! – won't it? How I shall laugh! It will be so ridiculous to see all his letters directed to him with an M.P. – But do you know, he says, he will never frank for me? He declares he won't. Don't you, Mr. Palmer?"

Mr. Palmer took no notice of her.

"He cannot bear writing, you know," she

continued – ”he says it is quite shocking.”

“No,” said he, “I never said any thing so irrational. Don’t palm all your abuses of languages upon me.”

“There now; you see how droll he is. This is always the way with him! Sometimes he won’t speak to me for half a day together, and then he comes out with something so droll – all about any thing in the world.”

She surprised Elinor very much as they returned into the drawing-room, by asking her whether she did not like Mr. Palmer excessively.

“Certainly,” said Elinor; “he seems very agreeable.”

“Well – I am so glad you do. I thought you would, he is so pleasant; and Mr. Palmer is excessively pleased with you and your sisters I can tell you, and you can’t think how disappointed he will be if you don’t come to Cleveland. – I can’t imagine why you should object to it.”

Elinor was again obliged to decline her

invitation; and by changing the subject, put a stop to her entreaties. She thought it probable that as they lived in the same county, Mrs. Palmer might be able to give some more particular account of Willoughby's general character, than could be gathered from the Middletons' partial acquaintance with him; and she was eager to gain from any one, such a confirmation of his merits as might remove the possibility of fear from Marianne. She began by inquiring if they saw much of Mr. Willoughby at Cleveland, and whether they were intimately acquainted with him.

"Oh dear, yes; I know him extremely well," replied Mrs. Palmer; – "Not that I ever spoke to him, indeed; but I have seen him for ever in town. Somehow or other I never happened to be staying at Barton while he was at Allenham. Mama saw him here once before; – but I was with my uncle at Weymouth. However, I dare say we should have seen a great deal of him in Somersetshire, if it had not happened very unluckily that we should never have been in the country together. He is very little at Combe, I believe; but if he were ever so much there, I do not think Mr. Palmer would visit him, for he is in the opposition, you know, and besides it is such a way off. I know why you inquire about him, very well; your sister is to marry him. I am monstrous glad of it, for then I shall have her for a neighbour you know."

"Upon my word," replied Elinor, "you know much more of the matter than I do, if you have any reason to expect such a match."

"Don't pretend to deny it, because you know it is what every body talks of. I assure you I heard of it in my way through town."

"My dear Mrs. Palmer!"

"Upon my honour I did. – I met Colonel Brandon Monday morning in Bond-street, just before we left town, and he told me of it directly."

"You surprise me very much. Colonel Brandon tell you of it! Surely you must be mistaken. To give such intelligence to a person who could not be interested in it, even if it were true, is not what I should expect Colonel Brandon to do."

"But I do assure you it was so, for all that, and I will tell you how it happened. When we met him, he turned back and walked with us; and so we began talking of my brother and sister, and one thing and another, and I said to him, 'So, Colonel, there is a new family come to Barton cottage, I hear, and mama sends me word they are very pretty, and that one of them is going to be married to Mr. Willoughby of Combe Magna. Is it true, pray? for of course you must know, as you have been in Devonshire so lately.'"

"And what did the Colonel say?"

"Oh – he did not say much; but he looked as if he knew it to be true, so from that moment I set it down as certain. It will be quite delightful, I declare! When is it to take place?"

"Mr. Brandon was very well I hope?"

"Oh! yes, quite well; and so full of your

praises, he did nothing but say fine things of you."

"I am flattered by his commendation. He seems an excellent man; and I think him uncommonly pleasing."

"So do I. – He is such a charming man, that it is quite a pity he should be so grave and so dull. Mama says **he** was in love with your sister too. – I assure you it was a great compliment if he was, for he hardly ever falls in love with any body."

"Is Mr. Willoughby much known in your part of Somersetshire?" said Elinor.

"Oh! yes, extremely well; that is, I do not believe many people are acquainted with him, because Combe Magna is so far off; but they all think him extremely agreeable I assure you. Nobody is more liked than Mr. Willoughby wherever he goes, and so you may tell your sister. She is a monstrous lucky girl to get him, upon my honour; not but that he is much more lucky in getting her, because she is so very handsome and agreeable, that nothing can be good enough for her. However, I don't think her hardly at all handsomer than you, I assure you; for I think you both excessively pretty, and so does Mr. Palmer too I am sure, though we could not get him to own it last night."

Mrs. Palmer's information respecting Willoughby was not very material; but any testimony in his favour, however small, was pleasing to her.

"I am so glad we are got acquainted at last," continued Charlotte. – "And now I hope we shall always be great friends. You can't think how much I longed to see you! It is so delightful that you should live at the cottage! Nothing can be like it, to be sure! And I am so glad your sister is going to be well married! I hope you will be a great deal at Combe Magna. It is a sweet place, by all accounts."

"You have been long acquainted with Colonel Brandon, have not you?"

"Yes, a great while; ever since my sister

married. – He was a particular friend of Sir John's. I believe," she added in a low voice, "he would have been very glad to have had me, if he could. Sir John and Lady Middleton wished it very much. But mama did not think the match good enough for me, otherwise Sir John would have mentioned it to the Colonel, and we should have been married immediately."

"Did not Colonel Brandon know of Sir John's proposal to your mother before it was made? Had he never owned his affection to yourself?"

"Oh, no; but if mama had not objected to it, I dare say he would have liked it of all things. He had not seen me then above twice, for it was before I left school. However, I am much happier as I am. Mr. Palmer is the kind of man I like."

CHAPTER TWENTY ONE

THE PALMERS RETURNED to Cleveland the next day, and the two families at Barton were again left to entertain each other. But this did not last long; Elinor had hardly got their last visitors out of her head, had hardly done wondering at Charlotte's being so happy without a cause, at Mr. Palmer's acting so simply, with good abilities, and at the strange unsuitableness which often existed between husband and wife, before Sir John's and Mrs. Jennings's active zeal in the cause of society, procured her some other new acquaintance to see and observe.

In a morning's excursion to Exeter, they had met with two young ladies, whom Mrs. Jennings had the satisfaction of discovering to be her relations, and this was enough for Sir John to invite them directly to the park, as soon as their present engagements at Exeter were over. Their engagements at Exeter instantly gave way before such an invitation, and Lady Middleton was thrown into no little alarm on the return of Sir John, by hearing that she was very soon to receive a visit from two girls whom she had never seen in her life, and of whose elegance, – whose tolerable gentility even, she could have no proof; for the assurances of her husband and mother on that subject went for nothing at all. Their being her relations too made it so much the worse; and Mrs. Jennings's attempts at consolation were therefore unfortunately founded, when she advised her daughter not to care about their being so fashionable; because they were all cousins and must put up with one another. As it was impossible, however, now to prevent their coming, Lady Middleton resigned herself to the idea of it, with all the philosophy of a well-bred woman, contenting herself with merely giving her husband a gentle reprimand on the subject five or six times every day.

The young ladies arrived: their appearance was by no means ungenteel or unfashionable. Their dress was very smart, their manners very civil, they were delighted with the house, and in raptures with the furniture, and they happened to be so doatingly fond of children that Lady Middleton's good opinion was engaged in their favour before they had been an hour at the Park. She declared them to be very agreeable girls indeed, which for her ladyship was enthusiastic admiration. Sir John's confidence in his own judgment rose with this animated praise, and he set off directly for the cottage to tell the Miss Dashwoods of the Miss Steeles' arrival, and to assure them of their being the sweetest girls in the world. From such commendation as this, however, there was not much to be learned; Elinor well knew that the sweetest girls in the world were to be met with in every part of England, under every possible variation of form, face, temper and understanding. Sir John wanted the whole family to walk to the Park directly and look at his guests. Benevolent, philanthropic man! It was painful to him even to keep a third cousin to himself.

"Do come now," said he – "pray come – you must come – I declare you shall come – You can't think how you will like them. Lucy is monstrous pretty, and so good humoured and agreeable! The children are all hanging about her already, as if she was an old acquaintance. And they both long to see you of all things, for they have heard at Exeter that you are the most beautiful creatures in the world; and I have told them it is all very true, and a great deal more. You will be delighted with them I am sure. They have brought the whole coach full of playthings for the children. How can you be so cross as not to come? Why they are your cousins, you know, after a fashion. **You** are my cousins, and they are my wife's, so you must be related."

But Sir John could not prevail. He could only obtain a promise of their calling at the Park within a day or two, and then left them in amazement at their indifference, to walk home and boast anew of their attractions to the Miss Steeles, as he had been already boasting of the Miss Steeles to them.

When their promised visit to the Park and consequent introduction to these young ladies took place, they found in the appearance of the eldest, who was nearly thirty, with a very plain and not a sensible face, nothing to admire; but in the other, who was not more than two or three and twenty, they acknowledged considerable beauty; her features were pretty, and she had a sharp quick eye, and a smartness of air, which though it did not give actual elegance or grace, gave distinction to her person. – Their manners were particularly civil, and Elinor soon allowed them credit for some kind of sense, when she saw with what constant and judicious attention they were making themselves agreeable to Lady Middleton. With her children they were in continual raptures, extolling their beauty, courting their notice, and humouring their whims; and such of their time as could be spared from the importunate demands which this politeness made on it, was spent in admiration of whatever her ladyship was doing, if she happened to be doing any thing, or in taking patterns of some elegant new dress, in which her appearance the day before had thrown them into unceasing delight. Fortunately for those who pay their court through such foibles, a fond mother, though, in pursuit of praise for her children, the most rapacious of human beings, is likewise the most credulous; her demands are exorbitant; but she will swallow any thing; and the excessive affection and endurance of the Miss Steeles towards her offspring were viewed therefore by Lady Middleton without the smallest surprise or distrust. She saw with maternal complacency all the impertinent encroachments and mischievous tricks to which her cousins submitted. She saw their sashes untied, their hair pulled about their ears, their work-bags searched, and their knives and scissors stolen away, and felt no doubt of its being a reciprocal enjoyment. It suggested no other surprise than that Elinor and Marianne should sit so composedly by, without claiming a share in what was passing.

"John is in such spirits today!" said she, on his taking Miss Steeles's pocket handkerchief, and throwing it out of window – "He is full of monkey tricks."

And soon afterwards, on the second boy's

violently pinching one of the same lady's fingers, she fondly observed, "How playful William is!"

"And here is my sweet little Annamaria," she added, tenderly caressing a little girl of three years old, who had not made a noise for the last two minutes; "And she is always so gentle and quiet – Never was there such a quiet little thing!"

But unfortunately in bestowing these embraces, a pin in her ladyship's head dress slightly scratching the child's neck, produced from this pattern of gentleness such violent screams, as could hardly be outdone by any creature professedly noisy. The mother's consternation was excessive; but it could not surpass the alarm of the Miss Steeles, and every thing was done by all three, in so critical an emergency, which affection could suggest as likely to assuage the agonies of the little sufferer. She was seated in her mother's lap, covered with kisses, her wound bathed with lavender-water, by one of the Miss Steeles, who was on her knees to attend her, and her mouth stuffed with sugar plums by the other. With such a reward for her tears, the child was too wise to cease crying. She still screamed and sobbed lustily, kicked her two brothers for offering to touch her, and all their united soothings were ineffectual till Lady Middleton luckily remembering that in a scene of similar distress last week, some apricot marmalade had been successfully applied for a bruised temple, the same remedy was eagerly proposed for this unfortunate scratch, and a slight intermission of screams in the young lady on hearing it, gave them reason to hope that it would not be rejected. – She was carried out of the room therefore in her mother's arms, in quest of this medicine, and as the two boys chose to follow, though earnestly entreated by their mother to stay behind, the four young ladies were left in a quietness which the room had not known for many hours.

"Poor little creatures!" said Miss Steele, as soon as they were gone. "It might have been a very sad accident."

"Yet I hardly know how," cried Marianne, "unless it had been under totally different circumstances. But this is the usual way of heightening alarm, where there is nothing to be alarmed at in reality."

"What a sweet woman Lady Middleton is!" said Lucy Steele.

Marianne was silent; it was impossible for her to say what she did not feel, however trivial the occasion; and upon Elinor therefore the whole task of telling lies when politeness required it, always fell. She did her best when thus called on, by speaking of Lady Middleton with more warmth than she felt, though with far less than Miss Lucy.

"And Sir John too," cried the elder sister, "what a charming man he is!"

Here too, Miss Dashwood's commendation, being only simple and just, came in without any eclat. She merely observed that he was perfectly good humoured and friendly.

"And what a charming little family they have! I never saw such fine children in my life. – I declare I quite doat upon them already, and indeed I am always distractedly fond of children."

"I should guess so," said Elinor, with a smile, "from what I have witnessed this morning."

"I have a notion," said Lucy, "you think the little Middletons rather too much indulged; perhaps they may be the outside of enough; but it is so natural in Lady Middleton; and for my part, I love to see children full of life and spirits; I cannot bear them if they are tame and quiet."

"I confess," replied Elinor, "that while I am at Barton Park, I never think of tame and quiet children with any abhorrence."

A short pause succeeded this speech, which was first broken by Miss Steele, who seemed very much disposed for conversation, and who now said rather abruptly, "And how do you like Devonshire, Miss Dashwood? I suppose you were very sorry to leave Sussex."

In some surprise at the familiarity of this question, or at least of the manner in which it was spoken, Elinor replied that she was.

"Norland is a prodigious beautiful place, is not it?" added Miss Steele.

"We have heard Sir John admire it excessively," said Lucy, who seemed to think some apology necessary for the freedom of her sister.

"I think every one **must** admire it," replied Elinor, "who ever saw the place; though it is not to be supposed that any one can estimate its beauties as we do."

"And had you a great many smart beaux there? I suppose you have not so many in this part of the world; for my part, I think they are a vast addition always."

"But why should you think," said Lucy, looking ashamed of her sister, "that there are not as many genteel young men in

Devonshire as Sussex?"

"Nay, my dear, I'm sure I don't pretend to say that there an't. I'm sure there's a vast many smart beaux in Exeter; but you know, how could I tell what smart beaux there might be about Norland; and I was only afraid the Miss Dashwoods might find it dull at Barton, if they had not so many as they used to have. But perhaps you young ladies may not care about the beaux, and had as lief be without them as with them. For my part, I think they are vastly agreeable, provided they dress smart and behave civil. But I can't bear to see them dirty and nasty. Now there's Mr. Rose at Exeter, a prodigious smart young man, quite a beau, clerk to Mr. Simpson, you know, and yet if you do but meet him of a morning, he is not fit to be seen. – I suppose your brother was quite a beau, Miss Dashwood, before he married, as he was so rich?"

"Upon my word," replied Elinor, "I cannot tell you, for I do not perfectly comprehend the meaning of the word. But this I can say, that if he ever was a beau before he married, he is one still for there is not the smallest alteration in him."

"Oh! dear! one never thinks of married men's being beaux – they have something else to do."

"Lord! Anne," cried her sister, "you can talk of nothing but beaux; – you will make Miss Dashwood believe you think of nothing else." And then to turn the discourse, she began admiring the house and the furniture.

This specimen of the Miss Steeles was enough. The vulgar freedom and folly of the eldest left her no recommendation, and as Elinor was not blinded by the beauty, or the shrewd look of the youngest, to her want of real elegance and artlessness, she left the house without any wish of knowing them better.

Not so the Miss Steeles. – They came from Exeter, well provided with admiration for the use of Sir John Middleton, his family, and all his relations, and no niggardly proportion was now dealt out to his fair cousins, whom they declared to be the most beautiful, elegant, accomplished, and agreeable girls they had ever beheld, and with whom they were particularly anxious to be better acquainted. – And to be better acquainted therefore, Elinor soon found was their inevitable lot, for as Sir John was entirely on the side of the Miss Steeles, their party would be too strong for opposition, and that kind of intimacy must be submitted to, which consists of sitting an hour or two together in the same room almost every day. Sir John could do no more; but he did not know that any more was required: to be together was, in his opinion, to be intimate, and while his continual schemes for their meeting were effectual, he had not a doubt of their being established friends.

To do him justice, he did every thing in his power to promote their unreserve, by making the Miss Steeles acquainted with whatever he knew or supposed of his cousins' situations in the most delicate particulars, – and Elinor had not seen them more than twice, before the eldest of them wished her joy on her sister's having been so lucky as to make a conquest of a very smart beau since she came to Barton.

"'Twill be a fine thing to have her married so young to be sure," said she, "and I hear he is quite a beau, and prodigious handsome. And I hope you may have as good luck yourself soon, – but perhaps you may have a friend in the corner already."

Elinor could not suppose that Sir John would be more nice in proclaiming his suspicions of her regard for Edward, than he had been with respect to Marianne; indeed it was rather his favourite joke of the two, as being somewhat newer and more conjectural; and since Edward's visit, they had never dined together without his drinking to her best affections with so much significancy and so many nods and winks, as to excite general attention. The letter F – had been likewise invariably brought forward, and found productive of such countless jokes, that its character as the wittiest letter in the alphabet had been long established with Elinor.

The Miss Steeles, as she expected, had now all the benefit of these jokes, and in the eldest of them they raised a curiosity to know the name of the gentleman alluded to, which, though often impertinently expressed, was perfectly of a piece with her general inquisitiveness into the concerns of their family. But Sir John did not sport long with the curiosity which he delighted to raise, for he had at least as much pleasure in telling the name, as Miss Steele had in hearing it.

“His name is Ferrars,” said he, in a very audible whisper; “but pray do not tell it, for it's a great secret.”

“Ferrars!” repeated Miss Steele; “Mr.

Ferrars is the happy man, is he? What! your sister-in-law's brother, Miss Dashwood? a very agreeable young man to be sure; I know him very well."

"How can you say so, Anne?" cried Lucy, who generally made an amendment to all her sister's assertions. "Though we have seen him once or twice at my uncle's, it is rather too much to pretend to know him very well."

Elinor heard all this with attention and surprise. "And who was this uncle? Where did he live? How came they acquainted?" She wished very much to have the subject continued, though she did not chuse to join in it herself; but nothing more of it was said, and for the first time in her life, she thought Mrs. Jennings deficient either in curiosity after petty information, or in a disposition to communicate it. The manner in which Miss Steele had spoken of Edward, increased her curiosity; for it struck her as being rather ill-natured, and suggested the suspicion of that lady's knowing, or fancying herself to know something to his disadvantage. – But her curiosity was unavailing, for no farther notice was taken of Mr. Ferrars's name by Miss Steele when alluded to, or even openly mentioned by Sir John.

CHAPTER TWENTY TWO

MARIANNE, WHO HAD NEVER much toleration for any thing like impertinence, vulgarity, inferiority of parts, or even difference of taste from herself, was at this time particularly ill-disposed, from the state of her spirits, to be pleased with the Miss Steeles, or to encourage their advances; and to the invariable coldness of her behaviour towards them, which checked every endeavour at intimacy on their side, Elinor principally attributed that preference of herself which soon became evident in the manners of both, but especially of Lucy, who missed no opportunity of engaging her in conversation, or of striving to improve their acquaintance by an easy and frank communication of her sentiments.

Lucy was naturally clever; her remarks were often just and amusing; and as a companion for half an hour Elinor frequently found her agreeable; but her powers had received no aid from education: she was ignorant and illiterate; and her deficiency of all mental improvement, her want of information in the most common particulars, could not be concealed from Miss Dashwood, in spite of her constant endeavour to appear to advantage. Elinor saw, and pitied her for, the neglect of abilities which education might have rendered so respectable; but she saw, with less tenderness of feeling, the thorough want of delicacy, of rectitude, and integrity of mind, which her attentions, her assiduities, her flatteries at the Park betrayed; and she could have no lasting satisfaction in the company of a person who joined insincerity with ignorance; whose want of instruction prevented their meeting in conversation on terms of equality, and whose conduct toward others made every shew of attention and deference towards herself perfectly valueless.

"You will think my question an odd one, I dare say," said Lucy to her one day, as they were walking together from the park to the cottage – "but pray, are you personally acquainted with your sister-in-law's mother, Mrs. Ferrars?"

Elinor **did** think the question a very odd one, and her countenance expressed it, as she answered that she had never seen Mrs. Ferrars.

"Indeed!" replied Lucy; "I wonder at that, for I thought you must have seen her at Norland sometimes. Then, perhaps, you cannot tell me what sort of a woman she is?"

"No," returned Elinor, cautious of giving her real opinion of Edward's mother, and not very desirous of satisfying what seemed impertinent curiosity – "I know nothing of her."

"I am sure you think me very strange, for enquiring about her in such a way," said Lucy, eyeing Elinor attentively as she spoke; "but perhaps there may be reasons – I wish I might venture; but however I hope you will do me the justice of believing that I do not mean to be impertinent."

Elinor made her a civil reply, and they walked on for a few minutes in silence. It was broken by Lucy, who renewed the subject again by saying, with some hesitation,

"I cannot bear to have you think me impertinently curious. I am sure I would rather do any thing in the world than be thought so by a person whose good opinion is so well worth having as yours. And I am sure I should not have the smallest fear of trusting **you**; indeed, I should be very glad of your advice how to manage in such an uncomfortable situation as I am; but, however, there is no occasion to trouble **you**. I am sorry you do not happen to know Mrs. Ferrars."

"I am sorry I do **not**," said Elinor, in great astonishment, "if it could be of any use to **you** to know my opinion of her. But really I never understood that you were at all connected with that family, and therefore I am a little surprised, I confess, at so serious an inquiry into her character."

"I dare say you are, and I am sure I do not at all wonder at it. But if I dared tell you all, you would not be so much surprised. Mrs. Ferrars is certainly nothing to me at present – but the time **may** come – how soon it will come must depend upon herself – when we may be very intimately connected."

She looked down as she said this, amiably bashful, with only one side glance at her companion to observe its effect on her.

"Good heavens!" cried Elinor, "what do you

mean? Are you acquainted with Mr. Robert Ferrars? Can you be?" And she did not feel much delighted with the idea of such a sister-in-law.

"No," replied Lucy, "not to Mr. **Robert** Ferrars – I never saw him in my life; but," fixing her eyes upon Elinor, "to his eldest brother."

What felt Elinor at that moment? Astonishment, that would have been as painful as it was strong, had not an immediate disbelief of the assertion attended it. She turned towards Lucy in silent amazement, unable to divine the reason or object of such a declaration; and though her complexion varied, she stood firm in incredulity, and felt in no danger of an hysterical fit, or a swoon.

"You may well be surprised," continued Lucy; "for to be sure you could have had no idea of it before; for I dare say he never dropped the smallest hint of it to you or any of your family; because it was always meant to be a great secret, and I am sure has been faithfully kept so by me to this hour. Not a soul of all my relations know of it but Anne, and I never should have mentioned it to you, if I had not felt the greatest dependence in the world upon your secrecy; and I really thought my behaviour in asking so many questions about Mrs. Ferrars must seem so odd, that it ought to be explained. And I do not think Mr. Ferrars can be displeased, when he knows I have trusted you, because I know he has the highest opinion in the world of all your family, and looks upon yourself and the other Miss Dashwoods quite as his own sisters." – She paused.

Elinor for a few moments remained silent. Her astonishment at what she heard was at first too great for words; but at length forcing herself to speak, and to speak cautiously, she said, with calmness of manner, which tolerably well concealed her surprise and solicitude – "May I ask if your engagement is of long standing?"

"We have been engaged these four years."

"Four years!"

"Yes."

Elinor, though greatly shocked, still felt unable to believe it.

"I did not know," said she, "that you were even acquainted till the other day."

"Our acquaintance, however, is of many years date. He was under my uncle's care, you know, a considerable while."

"Your uncle!"

"Yes; Mr. Pratt. Did you never hear him talk of Mr. Pratt?"

"I think I have," replied Elinor, with an exertion of spirits, which increased with her increase of emotion.

"He was four years with my uncle, who lives at Longstaple, near Plymouth. It was there our acquaintance begun, for my sister and me was often staying with my uncle, and it was there our engagement was formed, though not till a year after he had quitted as a pupil; but he was almost always with us afterwards. I was very unwilling to enter into it, as you may imagine, without the knowledge and approbation of his mother; but I was too young, and loved him too well, to be so prudent as I ought to have been. – Though you do not know him so well as me, Miss Dashwood, you must have seen enough of him to be sensible he is very capable of making a woman sincerely attached to him."

"Certainly," answered Elinor, without knowing what she said; but after a moment's reflection, she added, with revived security of Edward's honour and love, and her companion's falsehood – "Engaged to Mr. Edward Ferrars! – I confess myself so totally surprised at what you tell me, that really – I beg your pardon; but surely there must be some mistake of person or name. We cannot mean the same Mr. Ferrars."

"We can mean no other," cried Lucy, smiling. "Mr. Edward Ferrars, the eldest son of Mrs. Ferrars, of Park Street, and brother of your sister-in-law, Mrs. John Dashwood, is the person I mean; you must allow that I am not likely to be deceived as to the name of the man on who all my happiness depends."

"It is strange," replied Elinor, in a most painful perplexity, "that I should never have heard him even mention your name."

"No; considering our situation, it was not strange. Our first care has been to keep the matter secret. – You knew nothing of me, or my family, and, therefore, there could be no **occasion** for ever mentioning my name to you; and, as he was always particularly afraid of his sister's suspecting any thing, **that** was reason enough for his not mentioning it."

She was silent. – Elinor's security sunk; but her self-command did not sink with it.

"Four years you have been engaged," said she with a firm voice.

"Yes; and heaven knows how much longer we may have to wait. Poor Edward! It puts him quite out of heart." Then taking a small miniature from her pocket, she added, "To prevent the possibility of mistake, be so good as to look at this face. It does not do him justice, to be sure, but yet I think you cannot be deceived as to the person it was drew for. – I have had it above these three years."

She put it into her hands as she spoke; and when Elinor saw the painting, whatever other doubts her fear of a too hasty decision, or her wish of detecting falsehood might suffer to linger in her mind, she could have none of its being Edward's face. She returned it almost instantly, acknowledging the likeness.

"I have never been able," continued Lucy, "to give him my picture in return, which I am very much vexed at, for he has been always so anxious to get it! But I am determined to set for it the very first opportunity."

"You are quite in the right," replied Elinor calmly. They then proceeded a few paces in silence. Lucy spoke first.

"I am sure," said she, "I have no doubt in the world of your faithfully keeping this secret, because you must know of what importance it is to us, not to have it reach his mother; for she would never approve of it, I dare say. I shall have no fortune, and I fancy she is an exceeding proud woman."

"I certainly did not seek your confidence," said Elinor; "but you do me no more than justice in imagining that I may be depended on. Your secret is safe with me; but pardon me if I express some surprise at so unnecessary a communication. You must at least have felt that my being acquainted with it could not add to its safety."

As she said this, she looked earnestly at Lucy, hoping to discover something in her countenance; perhaps the falsehood of the greatest part of what she had been saying; but Lucy's countenance suffered no change.

"I was afraid you would think I was taking

a great liberty with you," said she, "in telling you all this. I have not known you long to be sure, personally at least, but I have known you and all your family by description a great while; and as soon as I saw you, I felt almost as if you was an old acquaintance. Besides in the present case, I really thought some explanation was due to you after my making such particular inquiries about Edward's mother; and I am so unfortunate, that I have not a creature whose advice I can ask. Anne is the only person that knows of it, and she has no judgment at all; indeed, she does me a great deal more harm than good, for I am in constant fear of her betraying me. She does not know how to hold her tongue, as you must perceive, and I am sure I was in the greatest fright in the world t'other day, when Edward's name was mentioned by Sir John, lest she should out with it all. You can't think how much I go through in my mind from it altogether. I only wonder that I am alive after what I have suffered for Edward's sake these last four years. Every thing in such suspense and uncertainty; and seeing him so seldom – we can hardly meet above twice a-year. I am sure I wonder my heart is not quite broke."

Here she took out her handkerchief; but Elinor did not feel very compassionate.

"Sometimes." continued Lucy, after wiping her eyes, "I think whether it would not be better for us both to break off the matter entirely." As she said this, she looked directly at her companion. "But then at other times I have not resolution enough for it. – I cannot bear the thoughts of making him so miserable, as I know the very mention of such a thing would do. And on my own account too – so dear as he is to me – I don't think I could be equal to it. What would you advise me to do in such a case, Miss Dashwood? What would you do yourself?"

"Pardon me," replied Elinor, startled by the question; "but I can give you no advice under such circumstances. Your own judgment must direct you."

"To be sure," continued Lucy, after a few minutes silence on both sides, "his mother must provide for him sometime or other; but poor Edward is so cast down by it! Did you not think him dreadful low-spirited when he was at Barton? He was so miserable when he left us at Longstaple, to go to you, that I was afraid you would think him quite ill."

"Did he come from your uncle's, then, when he visited us?"

"Oh, yes; he had been staying a fortnight with us. Did you think he came directly from town?"

"No," replied Elinor, most feelingly sensible of every fresh circumstance in favour of Lucy's veracity; "I remember he told us, that he had been staying a fortnight with some friends near Plymouth." She remembered too, her own surprise at the time, at his mentioning nothing farther of those friends, at his total silence with respect even to their names.

"Did not you think him sadly out of spirits?" repeated Lucy.

"We did, indeed, particularly so when he first arrived."

"I begged him to exert himself for fear you should suspect what was the matter; but it made him so melancholy, not being able to stay more than a fortnight with us, and seeing me so much affected. – Poor fellow! – I am afraid it is just the same with him now; for he writes in wretched spirits. I heard from him just before I left Exeter;" taking a letter from her pocket and carelessly showing the direction to Elinor. "You know his hand, I dare say, a charming one it is; but that is not written so well as usual. – He was tired, I dare say, for he had just filled the sheet to me as full as possible."

Elinor saw that it **was** his hand, and she could doubt no longer. This picture, she had allowed herself to believe, might have been accidentally obtained; it might not have been Edward's gift; but a correspondence between them by letter, could subsist only under a positive engagement, could be authorised by nothing else; for a few moments, she was almost overcome – her heart sunk within her, and she could hardly stand; but exertion was indispensably necessary; and she struggled so resolutely against the oppression of her feelings, that her success was speedy, and for the time complete.

"Writing to each other," said Lucy, returning the letter into her pocket, "is the only comfort we have in such long separations. Yes, I have one other comfort in his picture, but poor Edward has not even **that**. If he had but my picture, he says he should be easy. I gave him a lock of my hair set in a ring when he was at Longstaple last, and that was some comfort to him, he said, but not equal to a picture. Perhaps you might notice the ring when you saw him?"

"I did," said Elinor, with a composure of

voice, under which was concealed an emotion and distress beyond any thing she had ever felt before. She was mortified, shocked, confounded.

Fortunately for her, they had now reached the cottage, and the conversation could be continued no farther. After sitting with them a few minutes, the Miss Steeles returned to the Park, and Elinor was then at liberty to think and be wretched.

CHAPTER TWENTY THREE

HOWEVER SMALL ELINOR'S general dependence on Lucy's veracity might be, it was impossible for her on serious reflection to suspect it in the present case, where no temptation could be answerable to the folly of inventing a falsehood of such a description. What Lucy had asserted to be true, therefore, Elinor could not, dared not longer doubt; supported as it was too on every side by such probabilities and proofs, and contradicted by nothing but her own wishes. Their opportunity of acquaintance in the house of Mr. Pratt was a foundation for the rest, at once indisputable and alarming; and Edward's visit near Plymouth, his melancholy state of mind, his dissatisfaction at his own prospects, his uncertain behaviour towards herself, the intimate knowledge of the Miss Steeles as to Norland and their family connections, which had often surprised her, the picture, the letter, the ring, formed altogether such a body of evidence, as overcame every fear of condemning him unfairly, and established as a fact, which no partiality could set aside, his ill-treatment of herself. – Her resentment of such behaviour, her indignation at having been its dupe, for a short time made her feel only for herself; but other ideas, other considerations, soon arose. Had Edward been intentionally deceiving her? Had he feigned a regard for her which he did not feel? Was his engagement to Lucy an engagement of the heart? No; whatever it might once have been, she could not believe it such at present. His affection was all her own. She could not be deceived in that. Her mother, sisters, Fanny, all had been conscious of his regard for her at Norland; it was not an illusion of her own vanity. He certainly loved her. What a softener of the heart was this persuasion! How much could it not tempt her to forgive! He had been blamable, highly blamable, in remaining at Norland after he first felt her influence over him to be more than it ought to be. In that, he could not be defended; but if he had injured her, how much more had he injured himself; if her case were pitiable, his was hopeless. His imprudence had made her miserable for a while; but it seemed to have deprived himself of all chance of ever being otherwise. She might in time regain tranquillity; but **he**, what had he to look forward to? Could he ever be tolerably happy with Lucy Steele; could he, were his affection for herself out of the question, with his integrity, his delicacy, and well-informed mind, be satisfied with a wife like her – illiterate, artful, and selfish?

The youthful infatuation of nineteen would naturally blind him to everything but her beauty and good nature; but the four succeeding years – years, which if rationally spent, give such improvement to the understanding, must have opened his eyes to her defects of education, while the same period of time, spent on her side in inferior society and more frivolous pursuits, had perhaps robbed her of that simplicity which might once have given an interesting character to her beauty.

If in the supposition of his seeking to marry herself, his difficulties from his mother had seemed great, how much greater were they now likely to be, when the object of his engagement was undoubtedly inferior in connections, and probably inferior in fortune to herself. These difficulties, indeed, with a heart so alienated from Lucy, might not press very hard upon his patience; but melancholy was the state of the person by whom the expectation of family opposition and unkindness, could be felt as a relief!

As these considerations occurred to her in painful succession, she wept for him, more than for herself. Supported by the conviction of having done nothing to merit her present unhappiness, and consoled by the belief that Edward had done nothing to forfeit her esteem, she thought she could even now, under the first smart of the heavy blow, command herself enough to guard every suspicion of the truth from her mother and sisters. And so well was she able to answer her own expectations, that when she joined them at dinner only two hours after she had first suffered the extinction of all her dearest hopes, no one would have supposed from the appearance of the sisters, that Elinor was mourning in secret over obstacles which must divide her for ever from the object of her love, and that Marianne was internally dwelling on the perfections of a man, of whose whole heart she felt thoroughly possessed, and whom she expected to see in every carriage which drove near their house.

The necessity of concealing from her mother and Marianne, what had been entrusted in confidence to herself, though it obliged her to unceasing exertion, was no aggravation of Elinor's distress. On the contrary it was a relief to her, to be spared the communication of what would give such affliction to them, and to be saved likewise from hearing that condemnation of Edward, which would probably flow from the excess of their partial affection for herself, and which was more than she felt equal to support.

From their counsel, or their conversation, she knew she could receive no assistance, their tenderness and sorrow must add to her distress, while her self-command would neither receive encouragement from their example nor from their praise. She was stronger alone, and her own good sense so well supported her, that her firmness was as unshaken, her appearance of cheerfulness as invariable, as with regrets so poignant and so fresh, it was possible for them to be.

Much as she had suffered from her first conversation with Lucy on the subject, she soon felt an earnest wish of renewing it; and this for more reasons than one. She wanted to hear many particulars of their engagement repeated again, she wanted more clearly to understand what Lucy really felt for Edward, whether there were any sincerity in her declaration of tender regard for him, and she particularly wanted to convince Lucy, by her readiness to enter on the matter again, and her calmness in conversing on it, that she was no otherwise interested in it than as a friend, which she very much feared her involuntary agitation, in their morning discourse, must have left at least doubtful. That Lucy was disposed to be jealous of her appeared very probable: it was plain that Edward had always spoken highly in her praise, not merely from Lucy's assertion, but from her venturing to trust her on so short a personal acquaintance, with a secret so confessedly and evidently important. And even Sir John's joking intelligence must have had some weight. But indeed, while Elinor remained so well assured within herself of being really beloved by Edward, it required no other consideration of probabilities to make it natural that Lucy should be jealous; and that she was so, her very confidence was a proof. What other reason for the disclosure of the affair could there be, but that Elinor might be informed by it of Lucy's superior claims on Edward, and be taught to avoid him in future? She had little difficulty in understanding thus much of her rival's intentions, and while she was firmly resolved to act by her as every principle of honour and honesty directed, to combat her own affection for Edward and to see him as little as possible; she could not deny herself the comfort of endeavouring to convince Lucy that her heart was unwounded. And as she could now have nothing more painful to hear on the subject than had already been told, she did not mistrust her own ability of going through a repetition of particulars with composure.

But it was not immediately that an opportunity of doing so could be commanded, though Lucy was as well disposed as herself to take advantage of any that occurred; for the weather was not often fine enough to allow of their joining in a walk, where they might most easily separate themselves from the others; and though they met at least every other evening either at the park or cottage, and chiefly at the former, they could not be supposed to meet for the sake of conversation. Such a thought would never enter either Sir John or Lady Middleton's head; and therefore very little leisure was ever given for a general chat, and none at all for particular discourse. They met for the sake of eating, drinking, and laughing together, playing at cards, or consequences, or any other game that was sufficiently noisy.

One or two meetings of this kind had taken place, without affording Elinor any chance of engaging Lucy in private, when Sir John called at the cottage one morning, to beg, in the name of charity, that they would all dine with Lady Middleton that day, as he was obliged to attend the club at Exeter, and she would otherwise be quite alone, except her mother and the two Miss Steeles. Elinor, who foresaw a fairer opening for the point she had in view, in such a party as this was likely to be, more at liberty among themselves under the tranquil and well-bred direction of Lady Middleton than when her husband united them together in one noisy purpose, immediately accepted the invitation; Margaret, with her mother's permission, was equally compliant, and Marianne, though always unwilling to join any of their parties, was persuaded by her mother, who could not bear to have her seclude herself from any chance of amusement, to go likewise.

The young ladies went, and Lady Middleton was happily preserved from the frightful solitude which had threatened her. The insipidity of the meeting was exactly such as Elinor had expected; it produced not one novelty of thought or expression, and nothing could be less interesting than the whole of their discourse both in the dining parlour and drawing room: to the latter, the children accompanied them, and while they remained there, she was too well convinced of the impossibility of engaging Lucy's attention to attempt it. They quitted it only with the removal of the tea-things. The card-table was then placed, and Elinor began to wonder at herself for having ever entertained a hope of finding time for conversation at the park. They all rose up in preparation for a round game.

"I am glad," said Lady Middleton to Lucy,

"you are not going to finish poor little Annamaria's basket this evening; for I am sure it must hurt your eyes to work filigree by candlelight. And we will make the dear little love some amends for her disappointment to-morrow, and then I hope she will not much mind it."

This hint was enough, Lucy recollected herself instantly and replied, "Indeed you are very much mistaken, Lady Middleton; I am only waiting to know whether you can make your party without me, or I should have been at my filigree already. I would not disappoint the little angel for all the world: and if you want me at the card-table now, I am resolved to finish the basket after supper."

"You are very good, I hope it won't hurt your eyes – will you ring the bell for some working candles? My poor little girl would be sadly disappointed, I know, if the basket was not finished tomorrow, for though I told her it certainly would not, I am sure she depends upon having it done."

Lucy directly drew her work table near her and reseated herself with an alacrity and cheerfulness which seemed to infer that she could taste no greater delight than in making a filigree basket for a spoilt child.

Lady Middleton proposed a rubber of Casino to the others. No one made any objection but Marianne, who with her usual inattention to the forms of general civility, exclaimed, "Your Ladyship will have the goodness to excuse **me** – you know I detest cards. I shall go to the piano-forte; I have not touched it since it was tuned." And without farther ceremony, she turned away and walked to the instrument.

Lady Middleton looked as if she thanked heaven that **she** had never made so rude a speech.

"Marianne can never keep long from that instrument you know, ma'am," said Elinor, endeavouring to smooth away the offence; "and I do not much wonder at it; for it is the very best toned piano-forte I ever heard."

The remaining five were now to draw their cards.

"Perhaps," continued Elinor, "if I should happen to cut out, I may be of some use to Miss Lucy Steele, in rolling her papers for her; and there is so much still to be done to the basket, that it must be impossible I think for her labour singly, to finish it this evening. I should like the work exceedingly, if she would allow me a share in it."

"Indeed I shall be very much obliged to you for your help," cried Lucy, "for I find there is more to be done to it than I thought there was; and it would be a shocking thing to disappoint dear Annamaria after all."

"Oh! that would be terrible, indeed," said Miss Steele – "Dear little soul, how I do love her!"

"You are very kind," said Lady Middleton to Elinor; "and as you really like the work, perhaps you will be as well pleased not to cut in till another rubber, or will you take your chance now?"

Elinor joyfully profited by the first of these proposals, and thus by a little of that address which Marianne could never condescend to practise, gained her own end, and pleased Lady Middleton at the same time. Lucy made room for her with ready attention, and the two fair rivals were thus seated side by side at the same table, and, with the utmost harmony, engaged in forwarding the same work. The pianoforte at which Marianne, wrapped up in her own music and her own thoughts, had by this time forgotten that any body was in the room besides herself, was luckily so near them that Miss Dashwood now judged she might safely, under the shelter of its noise, introduce the interesting subject, without any risk of being heard at the card-table.

CHAPTER TWENTY FOUR

IN A FIRM, though cautious tone, Elinor thus began.

"I should be undeserving of the confidence you have honoured me with, if I felt no desire for its continuance, or no farther curiosity on its subject. I will not apologize therefore for bringing it forward again."

"Thank you," cried Lucy warmly, "for breaking the ice; you have set my heart at ease by it; for I was somehow or other afraid I had offended you by what I told you that

Monday."

"Offended me! How could you suppose so? Believe me," and Elinor spoke it with the truest sincerity, "nothing could be farther from my intention than to give you such an idea. Could you have a motive for the trust, that was not honourable and flattering to me?"

"And yet I do assure you," replied Lucy, her little sharp eyes full of meaning, "there seemed to me to be a coldness and displeasure in your manner that made me quite uncomfortable. I felt sure that you was angry with me; and have been quarrelling with myself ever since, for having took such a liberty as to trouble you with my affairs. But I am very glad to find it was only my own fancy, and that you really do not blame me. If you knew what a consolation it was to me to relieve my heart speaking to you of what I am always thinking of every moment of my life, your compassion would make you overlook every thing else I am sure."

"Indeed, I can easily believe that it was a very great relief to you, to acknowledge your situation to me, and be assured that you shall never have reason to repent it. Your case is a very unfortunate one; you seem to me to be surrounded with difficulties, and you will have need of all your mutual affection to support you under them. Mr. Ferrars, I believe, is entirely dependent on his mother."

"He has only two thousand pounds of his own; it would be madness to marry upon that, though for my own part, I could give up every prospect of more without a sigh. I have been always used to a very small income, and could struggle with any poverty for him; but I love him too well to be the selfish means of robbing him, perhaps, of all that his mother might give him if he married to please her. We must wait, it may be for many years. With almost every other man in the world, it would be an alarming prospect; but

Edward's affection and constancy nothing can deprive me of I know."

"That conviction must be every thing to you; and he is undoubtedly supported by the same trust in your's. If the strength of your reciprocal attachment had failed, as between many people, and under many circumstances it naturally would during a four years' engagement, your situation would have been pitiable, indeed."

Lucy here looked up; but Elinor was careful in guarding her countenance from every expression that could give her words a suspicious tendency.

"Edward's love for me," said Lucy, "has been pretty well put to the test, by our long, very long absence since we were first engaged, and it has stood the trial so well, that I should be unpardonable to doubt it now. I can safely say that he has never gave me one moment's alarm on that account from the first."

Elinor hardly knew whether to smile or

sigh at this assertion.

Lucy went on. “I am rather of a jealous temper too by nature, and from our different situations in life, from his being so much more in the world than me, and our continual separation, I was enough inclined for suspicion, to have found out the truth in an instant, if there had been the slightest alteration in his behaviour to me when we met, or any lowness of spirits that I could not account for, or if he had talked more of one lady than another, or seemed in any respect less happy at Longstaple than he used to be. I do not mean to say that I am particularly observant or quick-sighted in general, but in such a case I am sure I could not be deceived.”

“All this,” thought Elinor, “is very pretty; but it can impose upon neither of us.”

“But what,” said she after a short silence, “are your views? or have you none but that of waiting for Mrs. Ferrars’s death, which is a melancholy and shocking extremity? – Is her son determined to submit to this, and to all the tediousness of the many years of suspense in which it may involve you, rather than run the risk of her displeasure for a while by owning the truth?"

"If we could be certain that it would be only for a while! But Mrs. Ferrars is a very headstrong proud woman, and in her first fit of anger upon hearing it, would very likely secure every thing to Robert, and the idea of that, for Edward's sake, frightens away all my inclination for hasty measures."

"And for your own sake too, or you are carrying your disinterestedness beyond reason."

Lucy looked at Elinor again, and was silent.

"Do you know Mr. Robert Ferrars?" asked Elinor.

"Not at all – I never saw him; but I fancy he is very unlike his brother – silly and a great coxcomb."

"A great coxcomb!" repeated Miss Steele, whose ear had caught those words by a sudden pause in Marianne's music. – "Oh, they are talking of their favourite beaux, I dare say."

"No sister," cried Lucy, "you are mistaken there, our favourite beaux are **not** great coxcombs."

"I can answer for it that Miss Dashwood's is not," said Mrs. Jennings, laughing heartily; "for he is one of the modestest, prettiest behaved young men I ever saw; but as for Lucy, she is such a sly little creature, there is no finding out who **she** likes."

"Oh," cried Miss Steele, looking significantly round at them, "I dare say Lucy's beau is quite as modest and pretty behaved as Miss Dashwood's."

Elinor blushed in spite of herself. Lucy bit her lip, and looked angrily at her sister. A mutual silence took place for some time. Lucy first put an end to it by saying in a lower tone, though Marianne was then giving them the powerful protection of a very magnificent concerto –

"I will honestly tell you of one scheme which has lately come into my head, for bringing matters to bear; indeed I am bound to let you into the secret, for you are a party concerned. I dare say you have seen enough of Edward to know that he would prefer the church to every other profession; now my plan is that he should take orders as soon as he can, and then through your interest, which I am sure you would be kind enough to use out of friendship for him, and I hope out of some regard to me, your brother might be persuaded to give him Norland living; which I understand is a very good one, and the present incumbent not likely to live a great while. That would be enough for us to marry upon, and we might trust to time and chance for the rest."

"I should always be happy," replied Elinor, "to show any mark of my esteem and friendship for Mr. Ferrars; but do you not perceive that my interest on such an occasion would be perfectly unnecessary?

He is brother to Mrs. John Dashwood – **that** must be recommendation enough to her husband."

"But Mrs. John Dashwood would not much approve of Edward's going into orders."

"Then I rather suspect that my interest would do very little."

They were again silent for many minutes. At length Lucy exclaimed with a deep sigh,

"I believe it would be the wisest way to put an end to the business at once by dissolving the engagement. We seem so beset with difficulties on every side, that though it would make us miserable for a time, we should be happier perhaps in the end. But you will not give me your advice, Miss Dashwood?"

"No," answered Elinor, with a smile, which concealed very agitated feelings, "on such a subject I certainly will not. You know very well that my opinion would have no weight with you, unless it were on the side of your wishes."

"Indeed you wrong me," replied Lucy, with

great solemnity; "I know nobody of whose judgment I think so highly as I do of yours; and I do really believe, that if you was to say to me, 'I advise you by all means to put an end to your engagement with Edward Ferrars, it will be more for the happiness of both of you,' I should resolve upon doing it immediately."

Elinor blushed for the insincerity of Edward's future wife, and replied, "This compliment would effectually frighten me from giving any opinion on the subject had I formed one. It raises my influence much too high; the power of dividing two people so tenderly attached is too much for an indifferent person."

"'Tis because you are an indifferent person," said Lucy, with some pique, and laying a particular stress on those words, "that your judgment might justly have such weight with me. If you could be supposed to be biased in any respect by your own feelings, your opinion would not be worth having."

Elinor thought it wisest to make no answer to this, lest they might provoke each other to an unsuitable increase of ease and unreserve; and was even partly determined never to mention the subject again. Another pause therefore of many minutes' duration, succeeded this speech, and Lucy was still the first to end it.

"Shall you be in town this winter, Miss Dashwood?" said she with all her accustomary complacency.

"Certainly not."

"I am sorry for that," returned the other, while her eyes brightened at the information, "it would have gave me such pleasure to meet you there! But I dare say you will go for all that. To be sure, your brother and sister will ask you to come to them."

"It will not be in my power to accept their invitation if they do."

"How unlucky that is! I had quite depended upon meeting you there. Anne and me are to go the latter end of January to some relations who have been wanting us to visit them these several years! But I only go for the sake of seeing Edward. He will be there in February, otherwise London would have no charms for me; I have not spirits for it."

Elinor was soon called to the card-table by the conclusion of the first rubber, and the confidential discourse of the two ladies was therefore at an end, to which both of them submitted without any reluctance, for nothing had been said on either side to make them dislike each other less than they had done before; and Elinor sat down to the card table with the melancholy persuasion that Edward was not only without affection for the person who was to be his wife; but that he had not even the chance of being tolerably happy in marriage, which sincere affection on **her** side would have given, for self-interest alone could induce a woman to keep a man to an engagement, of which she seemed so thoroughly aware that he was weary.

From this time the subject was never revived by Elinor, and when entered on by Lucy, who seldom missed an opportunity of introducing it, and was particularly careful to inform her confidante, of her happiness whenever she received a letter from Edward, it was treated by the former with calmness and caution, and dismissed as soon as civility would allow; for she felt such conversations to be an indulgence which Lucy did not deserve, and which were dangerous to herself.

The visit of the Miss Steeles at Barton Park was lengthened far beyond what the first invitation implied. Their favour increased; they could not be spared; Sir John would not hear of their going; and in spite of their numerous and long arranged engagements in Exeter, in spite of the absolute necessity of returning to fulfill them immediately, which was in full force at the end of every week, they were prevailed on to stay nearly two months at the park, and to assist in the due celebration of that festival which requires a more than ordinary share of private balls and large dinners to proclaim its importance.

CHAPTER TWENTY FIVE

THOUGH MRS. JENNINGS was in the habit of spending a large portion of the year at the houses of her children and friends, she was not without a settled habitation of her own. Since the death of her husband, who had traded with success in a less elegant part of the town, she had resided every winter in a house in one of the streets near Portman Square. Towards this home, she began on the approach of January to turn her thoughts, and thither she one day abruptly, and very unexpectedly by them, asked the elder Misses Dashwood to accompany her. Elinor, without observing the varying complexion of her sister, and the animated look which spoke no indifference to the plan, immediately gave a grateful but absolute denial for both, in which she believed herself to be speaking their united inclinations. The reason alleged was their determined resolution of not leaving their mother at that time of the year. Mrs. Jennings received the refusal with some surprise, and repeated her invitation immediately.

"Oh, Lord! I am sure your mother can spare you very well, and I **do** beg you will favour me with your company, for I've quite set my heart upon it. Don't fancy that you will be any inconvenience to me, for I shan't put myself at all out of my way for you. It will only be sending Betty by the coach, and I hope I can afford **that**. We three shall be able to go very well in my chaise; and when we are in town, if you do not like to go wherever I do, well and good, you may always go with one of my daughters. I am sure your mother will not object to it; for I have had such good luck in getting my own children off my hands that she will think me a very fit person to have the charge of you; and if I don't get one of you at least well married before I have done with you, it shall not be my fault. I shall speak a good word for you to all the young men, you may depend upon it."

"I have a notion," said Sir John, "that Miss Marianne would not object to such a scheme, if her elder sister would come into it. It is very hard indeed that she should not have a little pleasure, because Miss Dashwood does not wish it. So I would advise you two, to set off for town, when you are tired of Barton, without saying a word to Miss Dashwood about it."

"Nay," cried Mrs. Jennings, "I am sure I shall be monstrous glad of Miss Marianne's company, whether Miss Dashwood will go or not, only the more the merrier say I, and

I thought it would be more comfortable for them to be together; because, if they got tired of me, they might talk to one another, and laugh at my old ways behind my back. But one or the other, if not both of them, I must have. Lord bless me! how do you think I can live poking by myself, I who have been always used till this winter to have Charlotte with me. Come, Miss Marianne, let us strike hands upon the bargain, and if Miss Dashwood will change her mind by and bye, why so much the better."

"I thank you, ma'am, sincerely thank you," said Marianne, with warmth: "your invitation has insured my gratitude for ever, and it would give me such happiness, yes, almost the greatest happiness I am capable of, to be able to accept it. But my mother, my dearest, kindest mother, – I feel the justice of what Elinor has urged, and if she were to be made less happy, less comfortable by our absence – Oh! no, nothing should tempt me to leave her. It should not, must not be a struggle."

Mrs. Jennings repeated her assurance that Mrs. Dashwood could spare them perfectly well; and Elinor, who now understood her sister, and saw to what indifference to almost every thing else she was carried by her eagerness to be with Willoughby again, made no farther direct opposition to the plan, and merely referred it to her mother's decision, from whom however she scarcely expected to receive any support in her endeavour to prevent a visit, which she could not approve of for Marianne, and which on her own account she had particular reasons to avoid. Whatever Marianne was desirous of, her mother would be eager to promote – she could not expect to influence the latter to cautiousness of conduct in an affair respecting which she had never been able to inspire her with distrust; and she dared not explain the motive of her own disinclination for going to London. That Marianne, fastidious as she was, thoroughly acquainted with Mrs. Jennings' manners, and invariably disgusted by them, should overlook every inconvenience of that kind, should disregard whatever must be most wounding to her irritable feelings, in her pursuit of one object, was such a proof, so strong, so full, of the importance of that object to her, as Elinor, in spite of all that had passed, was not prepared to witness.

On being informed of the invitation, Mrs. Dashwood, persuaded that such an excursion would be productive of much amusement to both her daughters, and perceiving through all her affectionate attention to herself, how much the heart of Marianne was in it, would not hear of their declining the offer upon **her** account; insisted on their both accepting it directly; and then began to foresee, with her usual cheerfulness, a variety of advantages that would accrue to them all, from this separation.

"I am delighted with the plan," she cried,

"it is exactly what I could wish. Margaret and I shall be as much benefited by it as yourselves. When you and the Middletons are gone, we shall go on so quietly and happily together with our books and our music! You will find Margaret so improved when you come back again! I have a little plan of alteration for your bedrooms too, which may now be performed without any inconvenience to any one. It is very right that you **should** go to town; I would have every young woman of your condition in life acquainted with the manners and amusements of London. You will be under the care of a motherly good sort of woman, of whose kindness to you I can have no doubt. And in all probability you will see your brother, and whatever may be his faults, or the faults of his wife, when I consider whose son he is, I cannot bear to have you so wholly estranged from each other."

"Though with your usual anxiety for our happiness," said Elinor, "you have been obviating every impediment to the present scheme which occurred to you, there is still one objection which, in my opinion, cannot be so easily removed."

Marianne's countenance sunk.

"And what," said Mrs. Dashwood, "is my dear prudent Elinor going to suggest? What formidable obstacle is she now to bring forward? Do let me hear a word about the expense of it."

"My objection is this; though I think very well of Mrs. Jennings's heart, she is not a woman whose society can afford us pleasure, or whose protection will give us consequence."

"That is very true," replied her mother, "but of her society, separately from that of other people, you will scarcely have any thing at all, and you will almost always appear in public with Lady Middleton."

"If Elinor is frightened away by her dislike of Mrs. Jennings," said Marianne, "at least it need not prevent **my** accepting her invitation.

I have no such scruples, and I am sure I could put up with every unpleasantness of that kind with very little effort."

Elinor could not help smiling at this display of indifference towards the manners of a person, to whom she had often had difficulty in persuading Marianne to behave with tolerable politeness; and resolved within herself, that if her sister persisted in going, she would go likewise, as she did not think it proper that Marianne should be left to the sole guidance of her own judgment, or that Mrs. Jennings should be abandoned to the mercy of Marianne for all the comfort of her domestic hours. To this determination she was the more easily reconciled, by recollecting that Edward Ferrars, by Lucy's account, was not to be in town before February; and that their visit, without any unreasonable abridgement, might be previously finished.

"I will have you **both** go," said Mrs. Dashwood; "these objections are nonsensical. You will have much pleasure in being in London, and especially in being together; and if Elinor would ever condescend to anticipate enjoyment, she would foresee it there from a variety of sources; she would, perhaps, expect some from improving her acquaintance with her sister-in-law's family."

Elinor had often wished for an opportunity of attempting to weaken her mother's dependence on the attachment of Edward and herself, that the shock might be less when the whole truth were revealed, and now on this attack, though almost hopeless of success, she forced herself to begin her design by saying, as calmly as she could, "I like Edward Ferrars very much, and shall always be glad to see him; but as to the rest of the family, it is a matter of perfect indifference to me, whether I am ever known to them or not."

Mrs. Dashwood smiled, and said nothing. Marianne lifted up her eyes in astonishment, and Elinor conjectured that she might as well have held her tongue.

After very little farther discourse, it was finally settled that the invitation should be fully accepted. Mrs. Jennings received the information with a great deal of joy, and many assurances of kindness and care; nor was it a matter of pleasure merely to her. Sir John was delighted; for to a man, whose prevailing anxiety was the dread of being alone, the acquisition of two, to the number of inhabitants in London, was something. Even Lady Middleton took the trouble of being delighted, which was putting herself rather out of her way; and as for the Miss Steeles, especially Lucy, they had never been so happy in their lives as this intelligence made them.

Elinor submitted to the arrangement which counteracted her wishes with less reluctance than she had expected to feel. With regard to herself, it was now a matter of unconcern whether she went to town or not, and when she saw her mother so thoroughly pleased with the plan, and her sister exhilarated by it in look, voice, and manner, restored to all her usual animation, and elevated to more than her usual gaiety, she could not be dissatisfied with the cause, and would hardly allow herself to distrust the consequence.

Marianne's joy was almost a degree beyond happiness, so great was the perturbation of her spirits and her impatience to be gone. Her unwillingness to quit her mother was her only restorative to calmness; and at the moment of parting her grief on that score was excessive. Her mother's affliction was hardly less, and Elinor was the only one of the three, who seemed to consider the separation as any thing short of eternal.

Their departure took place in the first week in January. The Middletons were to follow in about a week. The Miss Steeles kept their station at the park, and were to quit it only with the rest of the family.

CHAPTER TWENTY SIX

ELINOR COULD NOT FIND herself in the carriage with Mrs. Jennings, and beginning a journey to London under her protection, and as her guest, without wondering at her own situation, so short had their acquaintance with that lady been, so wholly unsuited were they in age and disposition, and so many had been her objections against such a measure only a few days before! But these objections had all, with that happy ardour of youth which Marianne and her mother equally shared, been overcome or overlooked; and Elinor, in spite of every occasional doubt of Willoughby's constancy, could not witness the rapture of delightful expectation which filled the whole soul and beamed in the eyes of Marianne, without feeling how blank was her own prospect, how cheerless her own state of mind in the comparison, and how gladly she would engage in the solicitude of Marianne's situation to have the same animating object in view, the same possibility of hope. A short, a very short time however must now decide what Willoughby's intentions were; in all probability he was already in town. Marianne's eagerness to be gone declared her dependence on finding him there; and Elinor was resolved not only upon gaining every new light as to his character which her own observation or the intelligence of others could give her, but likewise upon watching his behaviour to her sister with such zealous attention, as to ascertain what he was and what he meant, before many meetings had taken place. Should the result of her observations be unfavourable, she was determined at all events to open the eyes of her sister; should it be otherwise, her exertions would be of a different nature – she must then learn to avoid every selfish comparison, and banish every regret which might lessen her satisfaction in the happiness of Marianne.

They were three days on their journey, and Marianne's behaviour as they travelled was a happy specimen of what future complaisance and companionableness to Mrs. Jennings might be expected to be. She sat in silence almost all the way, wrapt in her own meditations, and scarcely ever voluntarily speaking, except when any object of picturesque beauty within their view drew from her an exclamation of delight exclusively addressed to her sister. To atone for this conduct therefore, Elinor took immediate possession of the post of civility which she had assigned herself, behaved with the greatest attention to Mrs. Jennings, talked with her, laughed with her, and listened to her whenever she could; and Mrs. Jennings on her side treated them both with all possible kindness, was solicitous on every occasion for their ease and enjoyment, and only disturbed that she could not make them choose their own dinners at the inn, nor extort a confession of their preferring salmon to cod, or boiled fowls to veal cutlets. They reached town by three o'clock the third day, glad to be released, after such a journey, from the confinement of a carriage, and ready to enjoy all the luxury of a good fire.

The house was handsome, and handsomely fitted up, and the young ladies were immediately put in possession of a very comfortable apartment. It had formerly been Charlotte's, and over the mantelpiece still hung a landscape in coloured silks of her performance, in proof of her having spent seven years at a great school in town to some effect.

As dinner was not to be ready in less than two hours from their arrival, Elinor determined to employ the interval in writing to her mother, and sat down for that purpose. In a few moments Marianne did the same. "I am writing home, Marianne," said Elinor; "had not you better defer your letter for a day or two?"

"I am **not** going to write to my mother," replied Marianne, hastily, and as if wishing to avoid any farther inquiry. Elinor said no more; it immediately struck her that she must then be writing to Willoughby; and the conclusion which as instantly followed was, that, however mysteriously they might wish to conduct the affair, they must be engaged. This conviction, though not entirely satisfactory, gave her pleasure, and she continued her letter with greater alacrity. Marianne's was finished in a very few minutes; in length it could be no more than a note; it was then folded up, sealed, and directed with eager rapidity. Elinor thought she could distinguish a large W in the direction; and no sooner was it complete than Marianne, ringing the bell, requested the footman who answered it to get that letter conveyed for her to the two-penny post. This decided the matter at once.

Her spirits still continued very high; but there was a flutter in them which prevented their giving much pleasure to her sister, and this agitation increased as the evening drew on. She could scarcely eat any dinner, and when they afterwards returned to the drawing room, seemed anxiously listening to the sound of every carriage.

It was a great satisfaction to Elinor that Mrs. Jennings, by being much engaged in her own room, could see little of what was passing. The tea things were brought in, and already had Marianne been disappointed more than once by a rap at a neighbouring door, when a loud one was suddenly heard which could not be mistaken for one at any other house, Elinor felt secure of its announcing Willoughby's approach, and Marianne, starting up, moved towards the door. Every thing was silent; this could not be borne many seconds; she opened the door, advanced a few steps towards the stairs, and after listening half a minute, returned into the room in all the agitation which a conviction of having heard him would naturally produce; in the ecstasy of her feelings at that instant she could not help exclaiming, "Oh, Elinor, it is Willoughby, indeed it is!" and seemed almost ready to throw herself into his arms, when Colonel Brandon appeared.

It was too great a shock to be borne with calmness, and she immediately left the room. Elinor was disappointed too; but at the same time her regard for Colonel Brandon ensured his welcome with her; and she felt particularly hurt that a man so partial to her sister should perceive that she experienced nothing but grief and disappointment in seeing him. She instantly saw that it was not unnoticed by him, that he even observed Marianne as she quitted the room, with such astonishment and concern, as hardly left him the recollection of what civility demanded towards herself.

"Is your sister ill?" said he.

Elinor answered in some distress that she was, and then talked of head-aches, low spirits, and over fatigues; and of every thing to which she could decently attribute her sister's behaviour.

He heard her with the most earnest attention, but seeming to recollect himself, said no more on the subject, and began directly to speak of his pleasure at seeing them in London, making the usual inquiries about their journey, and the friends they had left behind.

In this calm kind of way, with very little interest on either side, they continued to talk, both of them out of spirits, and the thoughts of both engaged elsewhere. Elinor wished very much to ask whether Willoughby were then in town, but she was afraid of giving him pain by any enquiry after his rival; and at length, by way of saying something, she asked if he had been in London ever since she had seen him last. “Yes,” he replied, with some embarrassment, “almost ever since; I have been once or twice at Delaford for a few days, but it has never been in my power to return to Barton.”

This, and the manner in which it was said, immediately brought back to her remembrance all the circumstances of his quitting that place, with the uneasiness and suspicions they had caused to Mrs. Jennings, and she was fearful that her question had implied much more curiosity on the subject than she had ever felt.

Mrs. Jennings soon came in. “Oh! Colonel,” said she, with her usual noisy cheerfulness, “I am monstrous glad to see you – sorry I could not come before – beg your pardon, but I have been forced to look about me a little, and settle my matters; for it is a long while since I have been at home, and you know one has always a world of little odd things to do after one has been away for any time; and then I have had Cartwright to settle with – Lord, I have been as busy as a bee ever since dinner! But pray, Colonel, how came you to conjure out that I should be in town today?"

"I had the pleasure of hearing it at Mr. Palmer's, where I have been dining."

"Oh, you did; well, and how do they all do at their house? How does Charlotte do? I warrant you she is a fine size by this time."

"Mrs. Palmer appeared quite well, and I am commissioned to tell you, that you will certainly see her to-morrow."

"Ay, to be sure, I thought as much. Well, Colonel, I have brought two young ladies with me, you see – that is, you see but one of them now, but there is another somewhere. Your friend, Miss Marianne, too – which you will not be sorry to hear. I do not know what you and Mr. Willoughby will do between you about her. Ay, it is a fine thing to be young and handsome. Well! I was young once, but I never was very handsome – worse luck for me. However, I got a very good husband, and I don't know what the greatest beauty can do more. Ah! poor man! he has been dead these eight years and better. But Colonel, where have you been to since we parted? And how does your business go on? Come, come, let's have no secrets among friends."

He replied with his accustomary mildness to all her inquiries, but without satisfying her in any. Elinor now began to make the tea, and Marianne was obliged to appear again.

After her entrance, Colonel Brandon became more thoughtful and silent than he had been before, and Mrs. Jennings could not prevail on him to stay long. No other visitor appeared that evening, and the ladies were unanimous in agreeing to go early to bed.

Marianne rose the next morning with recovered spirits and happy looks. The disappointment of the evening before seemed forgotten in the expectation of what was to happen that day. They had not long finished their breakfast before Mrs. Palmer's barouche stopped at the door, and in a few minutes she came laughing into the room: so delighted to see them all, that it was hard to say whether she received most pleasure from meeting her mother or the Miss Dashwoods again. So surprised at their coming to town, though it was what she had rather expected all along; so angry at their accepting her mother's invitation after having declined her own, though at the same time she would never have forgiven them if they had not come!

"Mr. Palmer will be so happy to see you," said she; "What do you think he said when he heard of your coming with Mama? I forget what it was now, but it was something so droll!"

After an hour or two spent in what her mother called comfortable chat, or in other words, in every variety of inquiry concerning all their acquaintance on Mrs. Jennings's side, and in laughter without cause on Mrs. Palmer's, it was proposed by the latter that they should all accompany her to some shops where she had business that morning, to which Mrs. Jennings and Elinor readily consented, as having likewise some purchases to make themselves; and Marianne, though declining it at first was induced to go likewise.

Wherever they went, she was evidently always on the watch. In Bond Street especially, where much of their business lay, her eyes were in constant inquiry; and in whatever shop the party were engaged, her mind was equally abstracted from every thing actually before them, from all that interested and occupied the others. Restless and dissatisfied every where, her sister could never obtain her opinion of any article of purchase, however it might equally concern them both: she received no pleasure from anything; was only impatient to be at home again, and could with difficulty govern her vexation at the tediousness of Mrs. Palmer, whose eye was caught by every thing pretty, expensive, or new; who was wild to buy all, could determine on none, and dawdled away her time in rapture and indecision.

It was late in the morning before they returned home; and no sooner had they entered the house than Marianne flew eagerly up stairs, and when Elinor followed, she found her turning from the table with a sorrowful countenance, which declared that no Willoughby had been there.

"Has no letter been left here for me since we went out?" said she to the footman who then entered with the parcels. She was answered in the negative. "Are you quite sure of it?" she replied. "Are you certain that no servant, no porter has left any letter or note?"

The man replied that none had.

"How very odd!" said she, in a low and

disappointed voice, as she turned away to the window.

"How odd, indeed!" repeated Elinor within herself, regarding her sister with uneasiness. "If she had not known him to be in town she would not have written to him, as she did; she would have written to Combe Magna; and if he is in town, how odd that he should neither come nor write! Oh! my dear mother, you must be wrong in permitting an engagement between a daughter so young, a man so little known, to be carried on in so doubtful, so mysterious a manner! I long to inquire; and how will **my** interference be borne."

She determined, after some consideration, that if appearances continued many days longer as unpleasant as they now were, she would represent in the strongest manner to her mother the necessity of some serious enquiry into the affair.

Mrs. Palmer and two elderly ladies of Mrs. Jennings's intimate acquaintance, whom she had met and invited in the morning, dined with them. The former left them soon after tea to fulfill her evening engagements; and Elinor was obliged to assist in making a whist table for the others. Marianne was of no use on these occasions, as she would never learn the game; but though her time was therefore at her own disposal, the evening was by no means more productive of pleasure to her than to Elinor, for it was spent in all the anxiety of expectation and the pain of disappointment. She sometimes endeavoured for a few minutes to read; but the book was soon thrown aside, and she returned to the more interesting employment of walking backwards and forwards across the room, pausing for a moment whenever she came to the window, in hopes of distinguishing the long-expected rap.

CHAPTER TWENTY SEVEN

"IF THIS OPEN WEATHER holds much longer," said Mrs. Jennings, when they met at breakfast the following morning, "Sir John will not like leaving Barton next week; 'tis a sad thing for sportsmen to lose a day's pleasure. Poor souls! I always pity them when they do; they seem to take it so much to heart."

"That is true," cried Marianne, in a cheerful voice, and walking to the window as she spoke, to examine the day. "I had not thought of that. This weather will keep many sportsmen in the country."

It was a lucky recollection, all her good spirits were restored by it. "It is charming weather for **them** indeed," she continued, as she sat down to the breakfast table with a happy countenance. "How much they must enjoy it! But" (with a little return of anxiety) "it cannot be expected to last long. At this time of the year, and after such a series of rain, we shall certainly have very little more of it. Frosts will soon set in, and in all probability with severity. In another day or two perhaps; this extreme mildness can hardly last longer – nay, perhaps it may freeze tonight!"

"At any rate," said Elinor, wishing to prevent Mrs. Jennings from seeing her sister's thoughts as clearly as she did, "I dare say we shall have Sir John and Lady Middleton in town by the end of next week."

"Ay, my dear, I'll warrant you we do. Mary always has her own way."

"And now," silently conjectured Elinor, "she will write to Combe by this day's post."

But if she **did**, the letter was written and sent away with a privacy which eluded all her watchfulness to ascertain the fact. Whatever the truth of it might be, and far as Elinor was from feeling thorough contentment about it, yet while she saw Marianne in spirits, she could not be very uncomfortable herself. And Marianne was in spirits; happy in the mildness of the weather, and still happier in her expectation of a frost.

The morning was chiefly spent in leaving cards at the houses of Mrs. Jennings's acquaintance to inform them of her being in town; and Marianne was all the time busy in observing the direction of the wind, watching the variations of the sky and imagining an alteration in the air.

"Don't you find it colder than it was in the morning, Elinor? There seems to me a very decided difference. I can hardly keep my hands warm even in my muff. It was not so yesterday, I think. The clouds seem parting too, the sun will be out in a moment, and we shall have a clear afternoon."

Elinor was alternately diverted and pained; but Marianne persevered, and saw every night in the brightness of the fire, and every morning in the appearance of the atmosphere, the certain symptoms of approaching frost.

The Miss Dashwoods had no greater reason to be dissatisfied with Mrs. Jennings's style of living, and set of acquaintance, than with her behaviour to themselves, which was invariably kind. Every thing in her household arrangements was conducted on the most liberal plan, and excepting a few old city friends, whom, to Lady Middleton's regret, she had never dropped, she visited no one to whom an introduction could at all discompose the feelings of her young companions. Pleased to find herself more comfortably situated in that particular than she had expected, Elinor was very willing to compound for the want of much real enjoyment from any of their evening parties, which, whether at home or abroad, formed only for cards, could have little to amuse her.

Colonel Brandon, who had a general invitation to the house, was with them almost every day; he came to look at Marianne and talk to Elinor, who often derived more satisfaction from conversing with him than from any other daily occurrence, but who saw at the same time with much concern his continued regard for her sister. She feared it was a strengthening regard. It grieved her to see the earnestness with which he often watched Marianne, and his spirits were certainly worse than when at Barton.

About a week after their arrival, it became certain that Willoughby was also arrived. His card was on the table when they came in from the morning's drive.

"Good God!" cried Marianne, "he has been

here while we were out." Elinor, rejoiced to be assured of his being in London, now ventured to say, "Depend upon it, he will call again tomorrow." But Marianne seemed hardly to hear her, and on Mrs. Jennings's entrance, escaped with the precious card.

This event, while it raised the spirits of Elinor, restored to those of her sister all, and more than all, their former agitation. From this moment her mind was never quiet; the expectation of seeing him every hour of the day, made her unfit for any thing. She insisted on being left behind, the next morning, when the others went out.

Elinor's thoughts were full of what might be passing in Berkeley Street during their absence; but a moment's glance at her sister when they returned was enough to inform her, that Willoughby had paid no second visit there. A note was just then brought in, and laid on the table.

"For me!" cried Marianne, stepping hastily forward.

"No, ma'am, for my mistress."

But Marianne, not convinced, took it instantly up.

"It is indeed for Mrs. Jennings; how provoking!"

"You are expecting a letter, then?" said Elinor, unable to be longer silent.

"Yes, a little – not much."

After a short pause. "You have no confidence in me, Marianne."

"Nay, Elinor, this reproach from **you** – you who have confidence in no one!"

"Me!" returned Elinor in some confusion; "indeed, Marianne, I have nothing to tell."

"Nor I," answered Marianne with energy, "our situations then are alike. We have neither of us any thing to tell; you, because you do not communicate, and I, because I conceal nothing."

Elinor, distressed by this charge of reserve in herself, which she was not at liberty to do away, knew not how, under such circumstances, to press for greater openness in Marianne.

Mrs. Jennings soon appeared, and the note being given her, she read it aloud. It was from Lady Middleton, announcing their arrival in Conduit Street the night before, and requesting the company of her mother and cousins the following evening. Business on Sir John's part, and a violent cold on her own, prevented their calling in Berkeley Street. The invitation was accepted; but when the hour of appointment drew near, necessary as it was in common civility to Mrs. Jennings, that they should both attend her on such a visit, Elinor had some difficulty in persuading her sister to go, for still she had seen nothing of Willoughby; and therefore was not more indisposed for amusement abroad, than unwilling to run the risk of his calling again in her absence.

Elinor found, when the evening was over, that disposition is not materially altered by a change of abode, for although scarcely settled in town, Sir John had contrived to collect around him, nearly twenty young people, and to amuse them with a ball. This was an affair, however, of which Lady Middleton did not approve. In the country, an unpremeditated dance was very allowable; but in London, where the reputation of elegance was more important and less easily attained, it was risking too much for the gratification of a few girls, to have it known that Lady Middleton had given a small dance of eight or nine couple, with two violins, and a mere side-board collation.

Mr. and Mrs. Palmer were of the party; from the former, whom they had not seen before since their arrival in town, as he was careful to avoid the appearance of any attention to his mother-in-law, and therefore never came near her, they received no mark of recognition on their entrance. He looked at them slightly, without seeming to know who they were, and merely nodded to Mrs. Jennings from the other side of the room. Marianne gave one glance round the apartment as she entered: it was enough – **he** was not there – and she sat down, equally ill-disposed to receive or communicate pleasure. After they had been assembled about an hour, Mr. Palmer sauntered towards the Miss Dashwoods to express his surprise on seeing them in town, though Colonel Brandon had been first informed of their arrival at his house, and he had himself said something very droll on hearing that they were to come.

"I thought you were both in Devonshire," said he.

"Did you?" replied Elinor.

"When do you go back again?"

"I do not know." And thus ended their discourse.

Never had Marianne been so unwilling to dance in her life, as she was that evening, and never so much fatigued by the exercise. She complained of it as they returned to Berkeley Street.

"Aye, aye," said Mrs. Jennings, "we know

the reason of all that very well; if a certain person who shall be nameless, had been there, you would not have been a bit tired: and to say the truth it was not very pretty of him not to give you the meeting when he was invited."

"Invited!" cried Marianne.

"So my daughter Middleton told me, for it seems Sir John met him somewhere in the street this morning." Marianne said no more, but looked exceedingly hurt. Impatient in this situation to be doing something that might lead to her sister's relief, Elinor resolved to write the next morning to her mother, and hoped by awakening her fears for the health of Marianne, to procure those inquiries which had been so long delayed; and she was still more eagerly bent on this measure by perceiving after breakfast on the morrow, that Marianne was again writing to Willoughby, for she could not suppose it to be to any other person.

About the middle of the day, Mrs. Jennings

went out by herself on business, and Elinor began her letter directly, while Marianne, too restless for employment, too anxious for conversation, walked from one window to the other, or sat down by the fire in melancholy meditation. Elinor was very earnest in her application to her mother, relating all that had passed, her suspicions of Willoughby's inconstancy, urging her by every plea of duty and affection to demand from Marianne an account of her real situation with respect to him.

Her letter was scarcely finished, when a rap foretold a visitor, and Colonel Brandon was announced. Marianne, who had seen him from the window, and who hated company of any kind, left the room before he entered it. He looked more than usually grave, and though expressing satisfaction at finding Miss Dashwood alone, as if he had somewhat in particular to tell her, sat for some time without saying a word. Elinor, persuaded that he had some communication to make in which her sister was concerned, impatiently expected its opening. It was not the first time of her feeling the same kind of conviction; for, more than once before, beginning with the observation of "your sister looks unwell to-day," or "your sister seems out of spirits," he had appeared on the point, either of disclosing, or of inquiring, something particular about her. After a pause of several minutes, their silence was broken, by his asking her in a voice of some agitation, when he was to congratulate her on the acquisition of a brother? Elinor was not prepared for such a question, and having no answer ready, was obliged to adopt the simple and common expedient, of asking what he meant? He tried to smile as he replied, "your sister's engagement to Mr. Willoughby is very generally known."

"It cannot be generally known," returned Elinor, "for her own family do not know it."

He looked surprised and said, "I beg your pardon, I am afraid my inquiry has been impertinent; but I had not supposed any secrecy intended, as they openly correspond, and their marriage is universally talked of."

"How can that be? By whom can you have heard it mentioned?"

"By many – by some of whom you know nothing, by others with whom you are most intimate, Mrs. Jennings, Mrs. Palmer, and the Middletons. But still I might not have believed it, for where the mind is perhaps rather unwilling to be convinced, it will always find something to support its doubts, if I had not, when the servant let me in today, accidentally seen a letter in his hand, directed to Mr. Willoughby in your sister's writing. I came to inquire, but I was convinced before I could ask the question. Is every thing finally settled? Is it impossible to-? But I have no right, and I could have no chance of succeeding. Excuse me, Miss Dashwood. I believe I have been wrong in saying so much, but I hardly know what to do, and on your prudence I have the strongest dependence. Tell me that it is all absolutely resolved on, that any attempt, that in short concealment, if concealment be possible, is all that remains."

These words, which conveyed to Elinor a direct avowal of his love for her sister, affected her very much. She was not immediately able to say anything, and even when her spirits were recovered, she debated for a short time, on the answer it would be most proper to give. The real state of things between Willoughby and her sister was so little known to herself, that in endeavouring to explain it, she might be as liable to say too much as too little. Yet as she was convinced that Marianne's affection for Willoughby, could leave no hope of Colonel Brandon's success, whatever the event of that affection might be, and at the same time wished to shield her conduct from censure, she thought it most prudent and kind, after some consideration, to say more than she really knew or believed. She acknowledged, therefore, that though she had never been informed by themselves of the terms on which they stood with each other, of their mutual affection she had no doubt, and of their correspondence she was not astonished to hear.

He listened to her with silent attention, and on her ceasing to speak, rose directly from his seat, and after saying in a voice of emotion, “to your sister I wish all imaginable happiness; to Willoughby that he may endeavour to deserve her,” – took leave, and went away.

Elinor derived no comfortable feelings from this conversation, to lessen the uneasiness of her mind on other points; she was left, on the contrary, with a melancholy impression of Colonel Brandon’s unhappiness, and was prevented even from wishing it removed, by her anxiety for the very event that must confirm it.

CHAPTER TWENTY EIGHT

NOTHING OCCURRED DURING the next three or four days, to make Elinor regret what she had done, in applying to her mother; for Willoughby neither came nor wrote. They were engaged about the end of that time to attend Lady Middleton to a party, from which Mrs. Jennings was kept away by the indisposition of her youngest daughter; and for this party, Marianne, wholly dispirited, careless of her appearance, and seeming equally indifferent whether she went or staid, prepared, without one look of hope or one expression of pleasure. She sat by the drawing-room fire after tea, till the moment of Lady Middleton's arrival, without once stirring from her seat, or altering her attitude, lost in her own thoughts, and insensible of her sister's presence; and when at last they were told that Lady Middleton waited for them at the door, she started as if she had forgotten that any one was expected.

They arrived in due time at the place of destination, and as soon as the string of carriages before them would allow, alighted, ascended the stairs, heard their names announced from one landing-place to another in an audible voice, and entered a room splendidly lit up, quite full of company, and insufferably hot. When they had paid their tribute of politeness by curtsying to the lady of the house, they were permitted to mingle in the crowd, and take their share of the heat and inconvenience, to which their arrival must necessarily add. After some time spent in saying little or doing less, Lady Middleton sat down to Cassino, and as Marianne was not in spirits for moving about, she and Elinor luckily succeeding to chairs, placed themselves at no great distance from the table.

They had not remained in this manner long, before Elinor perceived Willoughby, standing within a few yards of them, in earnest conversation with a very fashionable looking young woman. She soon caught his eye, and he immediately bowed, but without attempting to speak to her, or to approach Marianne, though he could not but see her; and then continued his discourse with the same lady. Elinor turned involuntarily to Marianne, to see whether it could be unobserved by her. At that moment she first perceived him, and her whole countenance glowing with sudden delight, she would have moved towards him instantly, had not her sister caught hold of her.

"Good heavens!" she exclaimed, "he is

there – he is there – Oh! why does he not look at me? why cannot I speak to him?"

"Pray, pray be composed," cried Elinor, "and do not betray what you feel to every body present. Perhaps he has not observed you yet."

This however was more than she could believe herself; and to be composed at such a moment was not only beyond the reach of Marianne, it was beyond her wish. She sat in an agony of impatience which affected every feature.

At last he turned round again, and regarded them both; she started up, and pronouncing his name in a tone of affection, held out her hand to him. He approached, and addressing himself rather to Elinor than Marianne, as if wishing to avoid her eye, and determined not to observe her attitude, inquired in a hurried manner after Mrs. Dashwood, and asked how long they had been in town. Elinor was robbed of all presence of mind by such an address, and was unable to say a word. But the feelings of her sister were instantly expressed. Her face was crimsoned over, and she exclaimed, in a voice of the greatest emotion, "Good God! Willoughby, what is the meaning of this? Have you not received my letters? Will you not shake hands with me?"

He could not then avoid it, but her touch seemed painful to him, and he held her hand only for a moment. During all this time he was evidently struggling for composure. Elinor watched his countenance and saw its expression becoming more tranquil. After a moment's pause, he spoke with calmness.

"I did myself the honour of calling in Berkeley Street last Tuesday, and very much regretted that I was not fortunate enough to find yourselves and Mrs. Jennings at home. My card was not lost, I hope."

"But have you not received my notes?" cried Marianne in the wildest anxiety. "Here is some mistake I am sure – some dreadful mistake. What can be the meaning of it?

Tell me, Willoughby; for heaven's sake tell me, what is the matter?"

He made no reply; his complexion changed and all his embarrassment returned; but as if, on catching the eye of the young lady with whom he had been previously talking, he felt the necessity of instant exertion, he recovered himself again, and after saying, "Yes, I had the pleasure of receiving the information of your arrival in town, which you were so good as to send me," turned hastily away with a slight bow and joined his friend.

Marianne, now looking dreadfully white, and unable to stand, sunk into her chair, and Elinor, expecting every moment to see her faint, tried to screen her from the observation of others, while reviving her with lavender water.

"Go to him, Elinor," she cried, as soon as she could speak, "and force him to come to me. Tell him I must see him again – must speak to him instantly. – I cannot rest – I shall not have a moment's peace till this is explained – some dreadful misapprehension or other. – Oh go to him this moment."

"How can that be done? No, my dearest Marianne, you must wait. This is not the place for explanations. Wait only till tomorrow."

With difficulty however could she prevent her from following him herself; and to persuade her to check her agitation, to wait, at least, with the appearance of composure, till she might speak to him with more privacy and more effect, was impossible; for Marianne continued incessantly to give way in a low voice to the misery of her feelings, by exclamations of wretchedness. In a short time Elinor saw Willoughby quit the room by the door towards the staircase, and telling Marianne that he was gone, urged the impossibility of speaking to him again that evening, as a fresh argument for her to be calm. She instantly begged her sister would entreat Lady Middleton to take them home, as she was too miserable to stay a minute longer.

Lady Middleton, though in the middle of a rubber, on being informed that Marianne was unwell, was too polite to object for a moment to her wish of going away, and making over her cards to a friend, they departed as soon the carriage could be found. Scarcely a word was spoken during their return to Berkeley Street. Marianne was in a silent agony, too much oppressed even for tears; but as Mrs. Jennings was luckily not come home, they could go directly to their own room, where hartshorn restored her a little to herself. She was soon undressed and in bed, and as she seemed desirous of being alone, her sister then left her, and while she waited the return of Mrs. Jennings, had leisure enough for thinking over the past.

That some kind of engagement had subsisted between Willoughby and Marianne she could not doubt, and that Willoughby was weary of it, seemed equally clear; for however Marianne might still feed her own wishes, **she** could not attribute such behaviour to mistake or misapprehension of any kind. Nothing but a thorough change of sentiment could account for it. Her indignation would have been still stronger than it was, had she not witnessed that embarrassment which seemed to speak a consciousness of his own misconduct, and prevented her from believing him so unprincipled as to have been sporting with the affections of her sister from the first, without any design that would bear investigation. Absence might have weakened his regard, and convenience might have determined him to overcome it, but that such a regard had formerly existed she could not bring herself to doubt.

As for Marianne, on the pangs which so unhappy a meeting must already have given her, and on those still more severe which might await her in its probable consequence, she could not reflect without the deepest concern. Her own situation gained in the comparison; for while she could **esteem** Edward as much as ever, however they might be divided in future, her mind might be always supported. But every circumstance that could embitter such an evil seemed uniting to heighten the misery of Marianne in a final separation from Willoughby – in an immediate and irreconcilable rupture with him.

CHAPTER TWENTY NINE

BEFORE THE HOUSE-MAID had lit their fire the next day, or the sun gained any power over a cold, gloomy morning in January, Marianne, only half dressed, was kneeling against one of the window-seats for the sake of all the little light she could command from it, and writing as fast as a continual flow of tears would permit her. In this situation, Elinor, roused from sleep by her agitation and sobs, first perceived her; and after observing her for a few moments with silent anxiety, said, in a tone of the most considerate gentleness,

"Marianne, may I ask-?"

"No, Elinor," she replied, "ask nothing; you will soon know all."

The sort of desperate calmness with which this was said, lasted no longer than while she spoke, and was immediately followed by a return of the same excessive affliction. It was some minutes before she could go on with her letter, and the frequent bursts of grief which still obliged her, at intervals, to withhold her pen, were proofs enough of her feeling how more than probable it was that she was writing for the last time to Willoughby.

Elinor paid her every quiet and unobtrusive attention in her power; and she would have tried to sooth and tranquilize her still more, had not Marianne entreated her, with all the eagerness of the most nervous irritability, not to speak to her for the world. In such circumstances, it was better for both that they should not be long together; and the restless state of Marianne's mind not only prevented her from remaining in the room a moment after she was dressed, but requiring at once solitude and continual change of place, made her wander about the house till breakfast time, avoiding the sight of every body.

At breakfast she neither ate, nor attempted to eat any thing; and Elinor's attention was then all employed, not in urging her, not in pitying her, nor in appearing to regard her, but in endeavouring to engage Mrs. Jennings's notice entirely to herself.

As this was a favourite meal with Mrs. Jennings, it lasted a considerable time, and they were just setting themselves, after it, round the common working table, when a letter was delivered to Marianne, which she eagerly caught from the servant, and, turning of a death-like paleness, instantly ran out of the room. Elinor, who saw as plainly by this, as if she had seen the direction, that it must come from Willoughby, felt immediately such a sickness at heart as made her hardly able to hold up her head, and sat in such a general tremour as made her fear it impossible to escape Mrs. Jennings's notice. That good lady, however, saw only that Marianne had received a letter from Willoughby, which appeared to her a very good joke, and which she treated accordingly, by hoping, with a laugh, that she would find it to her liking. Of Elinor's distress, she was too busily employed in measuring lengths of worsted for her rug, to see any thing at all; and calmly continuing her talk, as soon as Marianne disappeared, she said,

"Upon my word, I never saw a young woman so desperately in love in my life! **My** girls were nothing to her, and yet they used to be foolish enough; but as for Miss Marianne, she is quite an altered creature. I hope, from the bottom of my heart, he won't keep her waiting much longer, for it is quite grievous to see her look so ill and forlorn.

Pray, when are they to be married?"

Elinor, though never less disposed to speak than at that moment, obliged herself to answer such an attack as this, and, therefore, trying to smile, replied, "And have you really, Ma'am, talked yourself into a persuasion of my sister's being engaged to Mr. Willoughby? I thought it had been only a joke, but so serious a question seems to imply more; and I must beg, therefore, that you will not deceive yourself any longer. I do assure you that nothing would surprise me more than to hear of their being going to be married."

"For shame, for shame, Miss Dashwood! how can you talk so? Don't we all know that it must be a match, that they were over head and ears in love with each other from the first moment they met? Did not I see them together in Devonshire every day, and all day long; and did not I know that your sister came to town with me on purpose to buy wedding clothes? Come,

come, this won't do. Because you are so sly about it yourself, you think nobody else has any senses; but it is no such thing, I can tell you, for it has been known all over town this ever so long. I tell every body of it and so does Charlotte."

"Indeed, Ma'am," said Elinor, very seriously, "you are mistaken. Indeed, you are doing a very unkind thing in spreading the report, and you will find that you have though you will not believe me now."

Mrs. Jennings laughed again, but Elinor had not spirits to say more, and eager at all events to know what Willoughby had written, hurried away to their room, where, on opening the door, she saw Marianne stretched on the bed, almost choked by grief, one letter in her hand, and two or three others laying by her. Elinor drew near, but without saying a word; and seating herself on the bed, took her hand, kissed her affectionately several times, and then gave way to a burst of tears, which at first was scarcely less violent than Marianne's. The latter, though unable to speak, seemed to feel all the tenderness of this behaviour, and after some time thus spent in joint affliction, she put all the letters into Elinor's hands; and then covering her face with her handkerchief, almost screamed with agony. Elinor, who knew that such grief, shocking as it was to witness it, must have its course, watched by her till this excess of suffering had somewhat spent itself, and then turning eagerly to Willoughby's letter, read as follows:

"Bond Street, January.

"**My Dear Madam**,

"I have just had the honour of receiving your letter, for which I beg to return my sincere acknowledgments. I am much concerned to find there was anything in my behaviour last night that did not meet your approbation; and though I am quite at a loss to discover in what point I could be so unfortunate as to offend you, I entreat your forgiveness of what I can assure you to have been perfectly unintentional. I shall never reflect on my former acquaintance with your family in Devonshire without the most grateful pleasure, and flatter myself it will not be broken by any mistake or misapprehension of my actions. My esteem for your whole family is very sincere; but if I have been so unfortunate as to give rise to a belief of more than I felt, or meant to express, I shall reproach myself for not having been more guarded in my professions of that esteem. That I should ever have meant more you will allow to be impossible, when you understand that my affections have been long engaged elsewhere, and it will not be many weeks, I believe, before this engagement is fulfilled. It is with great regret that I obey your commands in returning the letters with which I have been honoured from you, and the lock of hair, which you so obligingly bestowed on me.

"I am, dear Madam,
"Your most obedient
"humble servant,
"**John Willoughby**."

With what indignation such a letter as this must be read by Miss Dashwood, may be imagined. Though aware, before she began it, that it must bring a confession of his inconstancy, and confirm their separation for ever, she was not aware that such language could be suffered to announce it; nor could she have supposed Willoughby capable of departing so far from the appearance of every honourable and delicate feeling – so far from the common decorum of a gentleman, as to send a letter so impudently cruel: a letter which, instead of bringing with his desire of a release any professions of regret, acknowledged no breach of faith, denied all peculiar affection whatever – a letter of which every line was an insult, and which proclaimed its writer to be deep in hardened villainy.

She paused over it for some time with indignant astonishment; then read it again and again; but every perusal only served to increase her abhorrence of the man, and so bitter were her feelings against him, that she dared not trust herself to speak, lest she might wound Marianne still deeper by treating their disengagement, not as a loss to her of any possible good but as an escape from the worst and most irremediable of all evils, a connection, for life, with an unprincipled man, as a deliverance the most real, a blessing the most important.

In her earnest meditations on the contents of the letter, on the depravity of that mind which could dictate it, and probably, on the very different mind of a very different person, who had no other connection whatever with the affair than what her heart gave him with every thing that passed, Elinor forgot the immediate distress of her sister, forgot that she had three letters on her lap yet unread, and so entirely forgot how long she had been in the room, that when on hearing a carriage drive up to the door, she went to the window to see who could be coming so unreasonably early, she was all astonishment to perceive Mrs. Jennings's chariot, which she knew had not been ordered till one. Determined not to quit Marianne, though hopeless of contributing, at present, to her ease, she hurried away to excuse herself from attending Mrs. Jennings, on account of her sister being indisposed. Mrs. Jennings, with a thoroughly good-humoured concern for its cause, admitted the excuse most readily, and Elinor, after seeing her safe off, returned to Marianne, whom she found attempting to rise from the bed, and whom she reached just in time to prevent her from falling on the floor, faint and giddy from a long want of proper rest and food; for it was many days since she had any appetite, and many nights since she had really slept; and now, when her mind was no longer supported by the fever of suspense, the consequence of all this was felt in an aching head, a weakened stomach, and a general nervous faintness. A glass of wine, which Elinor procured for her directly, made her more comfortable, and she was at last able to express some sense of her kindness, by saying,

"Poor Elinor! how unhappy I make you!"

"I only wish," replied her sister, "there were any thing I **could** do, which might be of comfort to you."

This, as every thing else would have been, was too much for Marianne, who could only exclaim, in the anguish of her heart, "Oh! Elinor, I am miserable, indeed," before her voice was entirely lost in sobs.

Elinor could no longer witness this torrent of unresisted grief in silence.

"Exert yourself, dear Marianne," she cried, "if you would not kill yourself and all who love you. Think of your mother; think of her misery while **you** suffer: for her sake you must exert yourself."

"I cannot, I cannot," cried Marianne; "leave me, leave me, if I distress you; leave me, hate me, forget me! but do not torture me so. Oh! how easy for those, who have no sorrow of their own to talk of exertion! Happy, happy Elinor, **you** cannot have an idea of what I suffer."

"Do you call **me** happy, Marianne? Ah! if you knew! – And can you believe me to be so, while I see you so wretched!"

"Forgive me, forgive me," throwing her arms round her sister's neck; "I know you feel for me; I know what a heart you have; but yet you are – you must be happy; Edward loves you – what, oh what, can do away such happiness as that?"

"Many, many circumstances," said Elinor, solemnly.

"No, no, no," cried Marianne wildly, "he loves you, and only you. You **can** have no grief."

"I can have no pleasure while I see you in

this state."

"And you will never see me otherwise. Mine is a misery which nothing can do away."

"You must not talk so, Marianne. Have you no comforts? no friends? Is your loss such as leaves no opening for consolation? Much as you suffer now, think of what you would have suffered if the discovery of his character had been delayed to a later period – if your engagement had been carried on for months and months, as it might have been, before he chose to put an end to it. Every additional day of unhappy confidence, on your side, would have made the blow more dreadful."

"Engagement!" cried Marianne, "there has been no engagement."

"No engagement!"

"No, he is not so unworthy as you believe him. He has broken no faith with me."

"But he told you that he loved you."

"Yes – no – never absolutely. It was every day implied, but never professedly declared.

Sometimes I thought it had been – but it never was."

"Yet you wrote to him?" –

"Yes – could **that** be wrong after all that had passed? – But I cannot talk."

Elinor said no more, and turning again to the three letters which now raised a much stronger curiosity than before, directly ran over the contents of all. The first, which was what her sister had sent him on their arrival in town, was to this effect.

Berkeley Street, January.

"How surprised you will be, Willoughby, on receiving this; and I think you will feel something more than surprise, when you know that I am in town. An opportunity of coming hither, though with Mrs. Jennings, was a temptation we could not resist. I wish you may receive this in time to come here to-night, but I will not depend on it. At any rate I shall expect you to-morrow. For the present, adieu.

"M.D."

Her second note, which had been written on the morning after the dance at the Middletons', was in these words: –

"I cannot express my disappointment in having missed you the day before yesterday, nor my astonishment at not having received any answer to a note which I sent you above a week ago. I have been expecting to hear from you, and still more to see you, every hour of the day. Pray call again as soon as possible, and explain the reason of my having expected this in vain. You had better come earlier another time, because we are generally out by one. We were last night at Lady Middleton's, where there was a dance. I have been told that you were asked to be of the party. But could it be so? You must be very much altered indeed since we parted, if that could be the case, and you not there. But I will not suppose this possible, and I hope very soon to receive your personal assurance of its being otherwise.

"M.D."

The contents of her last note to him were these: –

"What am I to imagine, Willoughby, by your behaviour last night? Again I demand an explanation of it. I was prepared to meet you with the pleasure which our separation naturally produced, with the familiarity which our intimacy at Barton appeared to me to justify. I was repulsed indeed! I have passed a wretched night in endeavouring to excuse a conduct which can scarcely be called less than insulting; but though I have not yet been able to form any reasonable apology for your behaviour, I am perfectly ready to hear your justification of it. You have perhaps been misinformed, or purposely deceived, in something concerning me, which may have lowered me in your opinion. Tell me what it is, explain the grounds on which you acted, and I shall be satisfied, in being able to satisfy you. It would grieve me indeed to be obliged to think ill of you; but if I am to do it, if I am to learn that you are not what we have hitherto believed you, that your regard for us all was insincere, that your behaviour to me was intended only to deceive, let it be told as soon as possible. My feelings are at present in a state of dreadful indecision; I wish to acquit you, but certainty on either side will be ease to what I now suffer. If your sentiments are no longer what they were, you will return my notes, and the lock of my hair which is in your possession.

"M.D."

That such letters, so full of affection and confidence, could have been so answered, Elinor, for Willoughby's sake, would have been unwilling to believe. But her condemnation of him did not blind her to the impropriety of their having been written at all; and she was silently grieving over the imprudence which had hazarded such unsolicited proofs of tenderness, not warranted by anything preceding, and most severely condemned by the event, when

Marianne, perceiving that she had finished the letters, observed to her that they contained nothing but what any one would have written in the same situation.

"I felt myself," she added, "to be as solemnly engaged to him, as if the strictest legal covenant had bound us to each other."

"I can believe it," said Elinor; "but unfortunately he did not feel the same."

"He **did** feel the same, Elinor – for weeks and weeks he felt it. I know he did. Whatever may have changed him now, (and nothing but the blackest art employed against me can have done it), I was once as dear to him as my own soul could wish. This lock of hair, which now he can so readily give up, was begged of me with the most earnest supplication. Had you seen his look, his manner, had you heard his voice at that moment! Have you forgot the last evening of our being together at Barton? The morning that we parted too! When he told me that it might be many weeks before we met again – his distress – can I ever forget his distress?"

For a moment or two she could say no more; but when this emotion had passed away, she added, in a firmer tone,

"Elinor, I have been cruelly used; but not by Willoughby."

"Dearest Marianne, who but himself? By whom can he have been instigated?"

"By all the world, rather than by his own heart. I could rather believe every creature of my acquaintance leagued together to ruin me in his opinion, than believe his nature capable of such cruelty. This woman of whom he writes – whoever she be – or any one, in short, but your own dear self, mama, and Edward, may have been so barbarous to bely me. Beyond you three, is there a creature in the world whom I would not rather suspect of evil than Willoughby, whose heart I know so well?"

Elinor would not contend, and only replied, "Whoever may have been so detestably your enemy, let them be cheated of their malignant triumph, my dear sister, by seeing how nobly the consciousness of your own innocence and good intentions supports your spirits. It is a reasonable and laudable pride which resists such malevolence."

"No, no," cried Marianne, "misery such as mine has no pride. I care not who knows that I am wretched. The triumph of seeing me so may be open to all the world. Elinor, Elinor, they who suffer little may be proud and independent as they like – may resist insult, or return mortification – but I cannot. I must feel – I must be wretched – and they are welcome to enjoy the consciousness of it that can."

"But for my mother's sake and mine – "

"I would do more than for my own. But to appear happy when I am so miserable – Oh! who can require it?"

Again they were both silent. Elinor was employed in walking thoughtfully from the fire to the window, from the window to the fire, without knowing that she received warmth from one, or discerning objects through the other; and Marianne, seated at the foot of the bed, with her head leaning against one of its posts, again took up Willoughby's letter, and, after shuddering over every sentence, exclaimed –

"It is too much! Oh, Willoughby, Willoughby, could this be yours! Cruel, cruel – nothing can acquit you. Elinor, nothing can. Whatever he might have heard against me – ought he not to have suspended his belief? ought he not to have told me of it, to have given me the power of clearing myself? 'The lock of hair, (repeating it from the letter,) which you so obligingly bestowed on me' – That is unpardonable. Willoughby, where was your heart when you wrote those words? Oh, barbarously insolent! – Elinor, can he be justified?"

"No, Marianne, in no possible way."

"And yet this woman – who knows what her art may have been? – how long it may have been premeditated, and how deeply contrived by her! – Who is she? – Who can she be? – Whom did I ever hear him talk of as young and attractive among his female acquaintance? – Oh! no one, no one – he talked to me only of myself."

Another pause ensued; Marianne was greatly agitated, and it ended thus.

"Elinor, I must go home. I must go and comfort mama. Can not we be gone to-morrow?"

"To-morrow, Marianne!"

"Yes, why should I stay here? I came only for Willoughby's sake – and now who cares for me? Who regards me?"

"It would be impossible to go to-morrow. We owe Mrs. Jennings much more than civility; and civility of the commonest kind must prevent such a hasty removal as that."

"Well then, another day or two, perhaps; but I cannot stay here long, I cannot stay to endure the questions and remarks of all these people. The Middletons and Palmers

– how am I to bear their pity? The pity of such a woman as Lady Middleton! Oh, what would **he** say to that!"

Elinor advised her to lie down again, and for a moment she did so; but no attitude could give her ease; and in restless pain of mind and body she moved from one posture to another, till growing more and more hysterical, her sister could with difficulty keep her on the bed at all, and for some time was fearful of being constrained to call for assistance. Some lavender drops, however, which she was at length persuaded to take, were of use; and from that time till Mrs. Jennings returned, she continued on the bed quiet and motionless.

CONTINUES IN VOLUME TWO

www.ingramcontent.com/pod-product-compliance
Lightning Source LLC
Chambersburg PA
CBHW020915310726
48980CB00011B/899/J

* 9 7 8 1 8 3 4 1 2 3 7 8 3 *